It's Terrific to Be Ten

It's Terrific to Be Ten

AN
APPLE
PAPERBACK

SCHOLASTIC INC.
New York   Toronto   London   Auckland   Sydney
Mexico City   New Delhi   Hong Kong

From THE KID IN THE RED JACKET by Barbara Park. Copyright © 1987 by Barbara Park. Reprinted by permission of Alfred A. Knopf Children's Books, a division of Random House, Inc. and Writer's House LLC.

From BUD, NOT BUDDY by Christopher Paul Curtis, copyright © 1999 by Christopher Paul Curtis. Used by permission of Random House Children's Books, a division of Random House, Inc.; and Charlotte Sheedy Literary Agency.

Excerpt from ANASTASIA KRUPNIK. Copyright © 1979 by Lois Lowry. Reprinted by permission of Houghton Mifflin Company. All rights reserved.

Reprinted with permission of Margaret K. McElderry Books, an imprint of Simon & Schuster Children's Publishing Division from YOLANDA'S GENIUS by Carol Fenner. Copyright © 1995 by Carol Fenner.

Reprinted with the permission of Atheneum Books for Young Readers, an imprint of Simon & Schuster Children's Publishing Division from BEETLES, LIGHTLY TOASTED by Phyllis Reynolds Naylor. Copyright © 1987 by Phyllis Reynolds Naylor.

From DEAR MR. HENSHAW by Beverly Cleary. Copyright © 1983 by Beverly Cleary. Used by permission of HarperCollins Publishers.

From IN THE YEAR OF THE BOAR AND JACKIE ROBINSON by Bette Bao Lord. Copyright © 1984 by Bette Bao Lord. Used by permission of HarperCollins Publishers.

From MY LIFE AS A FIFTH-GRADE COMEDIAN by Elizabeth Levy. Copyright © 1997 by Elizabeth Levy. Used by permission of HarperCollins Publishers.

From EVERYONE ELSE'S PARENTS SAID YES by Paula Danziger. Copyright © 1989 by Paula Danziger. Published by Delacorte Press, The Bantam Dell Publishing Group, A Division of Random House, Inc.

From BETSY AND TACY GO OVER THE BIG HILL by Maud Hart Lovelace. Copyright 1942 by Maud Hart Lovelace; copyright © renewed 1979 by Maud Hart Lovelace. Published by HarperCollins Publishers.

From BRIDGE TO TERABITHIA by Katherine Paterson. Copyright © 1977 by Katherine Paterson. Published by HarperCollins Publishers.

From AMY AND LAURA by Marilyn Sachs. Copyright © 1966 by Marilyn Sachs.

ISBN 0-439-21628-1

Copyright © 2000 by Scholastic Inc.

All rights reserved. Published by Scholastic Inc.
SCHOLASTIC, APPLE, and associated logos are trademarks
and/or registered trademarks of Scholastic Inc.

12 11 10 9 8 7 6 5 4 3   0 1 2 3 4 5/0

Printed in the U.S.A.   40

First Scholastic printing, November 2000

Contents

Introduction   vii

1. From *Beetles, Lightly Toasted*
   by Phyllis Reynolds Naylor   1

2. From *Anastasia Krupnik*
   by Lois Lowry   17

3. From *Everyone Else's Parents Said Yes*
   by Paula Danziger   39

4. From *Bud, Not Buddy*
   by Christopher Paul Curtis   51

5. From *Yolanda's Genius*
   by Carol Fenner   61

6. From *Dear Mr. Henshaw*
   by Beverly Cleary   76

7. From *In the Year of the Boar and
   Jackie Robinson* by Bette Bao Lord   85

8. From *Bridge to Terabithia*
   by Katherine Paterson   97

9. From *Betsy and Tacy Go Over the
   Big Hill* by Maud Hart Lovelace   103

10. From *My Life as a Fifth-Grade Comedian* by Elizabeth Levy   116

11. From *The Kid in the Red Jacket* by Barbara Park   124

12. From *Amy and Laura* by Marilyn Sachs   136

Introduction

Ten years old! An entire decade of life. "You have two numbers in your age when you are ten. It's the beginning of growing up," says Betsy Ray, in *Betsy and Tacy Go Over the Big Hill*.

Turning ten brings big changes. From that day on, you're more grown-up — whether you want to be or not. Here's your chance to read about all kinds of kids who have reached that double-digit year, in these twelve stories about ten-year-olds, excerpted from books by some of the best authors around.

You'll see ten-year-olds facing big problems on their own, like Shirley Temple Wong, the star of *In the Year of the Boar and Jackie Robinson*, who discovers that she can face the scary monsters in the basement of her apartment house. Or Leigh Botts, who asks his favorite author for help in *Dear Mr. Henshaw*, but ends up discovering that he can solve one of his biggest problems pretty well on his own. Bobby Garrick, in *My Life as a Fifth-Grade Comedian*, even manages to save himself from being kicked out of school.

You'll meet ten-year-olds setting big goals

for themselves. Sometimes the goals are serious: Yolanda, in *Yolanda's Genius,* takes on the challenge of helping her younger brother and succeeds. Sometimes the goals are less earthshaking: Andy Moller, in *Beetles, Lightly Toasted,* wants to get his name in the paper (and gets a lot more than he bargained for).

You'll see ten-year-olds dealing with friendship — trying to figure out what makes a best friend, like Amy Stern in *Amy and Laura;* struggling to make new friends in a new school, like Howard Jeeter in *The Kid in the Red Jacket;* or running into that girls-against-the-boys problem, like Matthew Martin, in *Everyone Else's Parents Said Yes.* And there's Jess Aarons, making a friend who changes his whole life, in *Bridge to Terabithia.*

There are ten-year-olds who've begun to crack the grown-up code, like Bud Caldwell in *Bud, Not Buddy,* and ten-year-olds who're busier solving the puzzle of their own ways of thinking, like Anastasia, in *Anastasia Krupnik.* Whatever they're facing, however they're coping, these kids really know what it's like to be ten — just the way you do. And isn't it terrific?

It's Terrific to Be Ten

From
Beetles, Lightly Toasted
by Phyllis Reynolds Naylor

Andy Moller has tied (with his cousin and rival Jack) for first place in the Roger B. Sudermann Essay Contest. Andy should be thrilled — but he's beginning to realize how much trouble he's in. The whole fifth-grade class is mad at him because they ate his worm and beetle recipes, but they had no idea what was really in them. Andy knows one way to set things right — but can he go through with it?

Andy got up from the table and answered the phone because he needed an excuse to leave. If he could have sailed out the window and over the treetops, he would have done so gladly. A ringing telephone was the next best thing. It saved him from simply getting up from the table and going upstairs to his room, which was what he was about to do anyway.

"Could I speak to Andy Moller, please?" said a man's voice at the other end.

"I'm Andy."

"Good! This is Frank Harris, a photographer from the *Bucksville Gazette*. Mr. Sudermann told me about you winning the essay contest — you and another boy — and we'd like to get a photo of the winners."

It was what Andy had been waiting for for two years — the reason he had entered the contest. Now, the last thing in the world he wanted was his picture in the *Bucksville Gazette,* but there was no way he could get out of it.

"You're the one who wrote about beetles and bugs, aren't you?" the photographer asked.

"Yes . . ."

"Well, what Mr. Sudermann has in mind, see, is a photo of you right there on the steps of the library eating one of those meals you wrote about."

Andy's arm went weak at the elbow and he almost dropped the receiver.

"You . . . you can't just take a picture of us standing on the steps?" he asked.

"Not much action in that. We're looking for a human-interest photo. Mr. Sudermann said he'll bring the chair and table on June tenth, and you bring your lunch. Okay? We got ourselves a deal?"

It was like being asked to go over Niagara

Falls in a barrel; to wade in a river with snakes. Eating a brownie without knowing there were beetles in it was bad enough, but sitting down to a meal of beetles, worms, and grubs, and *knowing* it was beyond anything he could imagine. The entire fifth-grade class was mad at him, however. He'd been a disappointment to Mrs. Haynes and his family too. Eating that meal himself was the only way that he could ever make up for what he'd done. He swallowed.

"Andy?" the photographer said.

Andy swallowed again. "Okay," he said. "I'll do it."

Then he hung up the phone and, with his family staring after him, went upstairs to his room.

No one but Jack spoke to him on the bus the next morning. Andy wondered why Jack bothered. He could have turned up his nose at Andy so easily, like everyone else was doing. Maybe, as Mother had said, Jack really *was* lonely, and knew how it felt.

At recess, however, Sam sat beside Andy on the steps, and Andy told him what the photographer had asked.

"Man, this sure turned out different than you thought," Sam said after they'd sat a while in silence. "What are you going to do?"

"I'm going to eat that lunch," Andy said.

Sam swallowed. "Maybe you just have to put your fork in it and *look* like you're eating," he suggested.

Andy shook his head. "That would be enough for the newspaper, but not for the people who were standing there watching."

Sam moaned as if in pain. "And you can't fake it," he said. "Just wouldn't be right. You've really got to put bugs in those brownies."

Andy nodded. He tried to think of what could be worse. If he had his choice of eating that lunch or breaking his leg, would he still rather break his leg? If someone told him he could walk down the street in his underpants or eat those beetles, would he still rather walk down the street in his underpants?

"It's all how you look at it," Sam said, still trying to help. "You know those dudes who walk over hot coals? You know how they sleep on nails? It's all up here," Sam said, tapping his forehead.

"So?" said Andy.

"So when it's time for you to eat those worms, you think applesauce — little tubes of applesauce — that's all you're eating. You get those beetles in your mouth, you think cornflakes."

"I'll try," said Andy.

That evening, as Andy helped his father with the milking, WMT played a song about a long-distance trucker who was running away from love, and then it was time for the eastern roundup — "News from our neighboring counties," the announcer said. Andy was only half listening as he rolled the big milk cans across the floor, but then the announcer said, ". . . and from Bucksville comes word that there are *two* winners this year in the annual Roger B. Sudermann Contest — one boy who cooks fish in the dishwasher and another who eats toasted beetles and worms. That's right, folks. In a contest rewarding ingenuity and imagination among fifth graders, these two boys propose to save energy and money by cooking in unusual ways and digging up food in the backyard." And here the announcer broke into a song: "Nobody loves me, everybody hates me, I guess I'll go eat worms." Then he laughed and said, "These boys are serious, though, and on June tenth, Jack Barth and Andy Moller each will receive an award and a check from Luther Sudermann, publisher of the *Bucksville Gazette,* who organized the contest in memory of his son. Congratulations, boys, but just don't invite me over for dinner, huh . . . ?"

Andy turned his back to the radio and sat down weakly on a bale of hay.

"Well, Andy," said his father, "you got yourself into this, and it wasn't such a bad idea — only the way you went about it. How do you figure to set things right?"

"I'm going to eat that stuff myself," Andy told him.

His father was quiet for a moment as he moved to another group of cows and attached the cups of the milking machine. "How d'you figure that's going to help?"

"I'm going to do it on the steps of the library," Andy said. "A photographer's going to take a picture of it. It was Mr. Sudermann's idea."

Andy couldn't quite tell if his father was laughing or not. There was certainly a smile in his voice when he said, "Well, I'll say this — it sure is going to make a lot of people awful happy."

Dad must have told Mother and she must have told Aunt Wanda, and after that, it was only a matter of time before Lois, Wayne, and Wendell heard about it and the whole of Bucksville besides. Lois, who had not spoken to Andy since the night she gargled in the sink, treated him more politely, cautiously, like a prisoner who was about to be shot.

The night before the award ceremony, Andy dreamed that he was eating spinach, only it was made of green worms — stringy worms — and he couldn't seem to swallow them; they just went halfway down his throat and then wouldn't go either way.

The next day Andy got up, did his chores in the barn, and went to the cellar for the last remaining frozen worms beneath his mother's pies. He set them on the kitchen counter along with the jar containing the last of the toasted beetle bits, then went out in the barn with a screwdriver to find a few more meal-worm grubs between the floorboards. Mother had taken Lois into town early for a haircut, and they would meet Andy on the steps of the library at noon before they did the rest of their errands. Dad and Wayne and Wendell were cultivating and wouldn't be able to come, but at least they would see Andy's picture in the paper, they told him.

Back in the kitchen, Andy had just got out the flour and chocolate for the brownies when he heard a voice behind him saying, "Need any help, Andy?"

Aunt Wanda came in the kitchen and put on her apron.

At first he was going to say no, but he didn't know much about deep-frying in fat.

"Well," he said, "I can make the brownies and the egg salad, but I'm not sure how to . . . uh . . ."

"Fry worms," said Aunt Wanda.

"Yeah," said Andy. "Sam fried them before in his dad's restaurant — just dropped them in the batter when his dad was frying chicken — but I didn't want to ask him again. . . ."

"Last thing in the world a new restaurant needs is a rumor going around that it fries worms," said Aunt Wanda. "If I can deep-fry chicken, I can deep-fry worms. Let me have them."

By eleven-thirty the lunch was packed in a brown paper bag, Andy had on his good trousers and shirt, and sat in the front seat of Wendell's pickup with Aunt Wanda at the wheel. There had been an announcement in the paper that morning that Andy would be eating his "conservation lunch" on the steps of the public library at twelve noon, and it listed the menu, which the reporter had jazzed up a bit:

Earthworms, en Brochette
Grub on Seeded Roll
Beetle Brownies

This is how it feels to go to war, Andy thought as they passed fields where corn was already ankle high and cows were munching contentedly in pastures. The clouds looked like swirls of whipped cream, and the breeze floating in the window carried the scent of clover. But it all seemed to be for someone else to enjoy, not Andy.

Aunt Wanda was surprisingly kind. Andy noticed that she had made his grub sandwich as attractive as possible, with a big piece of crisp lettuce and sesame roll. But Andy knew that even if she had served the roll on a silver platter with caramel sauce over the top, it still wouldn't have disguised what was in it.

His heart began to thump harder as the pickup turned down Main Street. It looked as though the entire fifth-grade class was there, plus their parents and a dozen other people besides. Mother and Lois were standing off to one side, Mother looking concerned. There was a card table and a folding chair at the bottom of the library steps, and a photographer stood nearby, talking with Mr. Sudermann. People were looking out of the door of the bank and from the upper windows of Owens Hardware.

Jack was already there with Aunt Bernadine, and when Andy walked up the steps beside him, Jack whispered, in awe,

"Andy, you really going to do it?"

"Yes," said Andy.

Mr. Sudermann gave the same speech he had given in the classroom, but this time he said that it was four years ago exactly that Roger fell off the silo, and in memory of his son's inquisitiveness and ingenuity, he was happy to present two awards this year to boys who had proved that a mind is capable of better things than simply watching TV.

"Farmers, and sons and daughters of farmers, after all, know the value of land, and the importance of thrift and conservation of all our natural resources. And so, with conservation as the theme this year, it is with great pleasure that I present Jack Barth with the Roger B. Sudermann award and a check for fifty dollars for his ideas on conserving energy by cooking in unusual ways with alternate sources of heat."

He handed Jack a little bronze pin that said "Imagination," then a check from his vest pocket, and finally he shook his hand.

"Congratulations," he said.

"Thank you," said Jack. The people clapped and the photographer snapped a picture.

"And it is with equally great pleasure that

I present Andy Moller with an award for his essay on unusual sources of food to provide fat and protein in the diet," Mr. Sudermann said. He gave Andy the other pin and the other check, then shook his hand also.

"Congratulations," he said.

"Thank you," said Andy, and again the people clapped and the photographer snapped his shutter.

Mr. Sudermann smiled down at Andy. "Well now, Andy, I believe you promised a demonstration of just how tasty your recipes can be."

The crowd smiled and pushed a little closer. Sam and Travers were there, and Sam looked worried. Russ Zumbach and Dora Kray were there in front too, grinning. They did not look worried. As Dad had said, this was going to make a lot of people very happy. Everyone was waiting for the main attraction.

Andy went to the card table and sat down. He took his lunch from out of the bag and spread it out before him on the card table. There was a muffled giggle from Jack, who had gone back to stand beside Aunt Bernie.

Andy unwrapped the deep-fried worms and set them on top the brown bag. Then he unwrapped the grub sandwich with the

Boston lettuce, and finally the chocolate brownie with the beetle backs glistening in the dough.

He tried to keep his jaw steady. *Tubes of applesauce,* Sam had said about the worms. The photographer was squatting down at eye level, tipping the camera. Jack giggled out loud this time, and Aunt Bernie poked him with her elbow.

Suddenly Andy looked up at Mr. Sudermann. "It doesn't seem right for me to enjoy this all by myself," he smiled. "Jack was a winner too. He can share it with me."

Jack's face went gray.

"Good idea!" said Mr. Sudermann, and to the photographer, "Get both of them in the picture. That's better yet."

Jack tried to protest that he wasn't hungry, but Mr. Owens from the hardware store picked up one of his empty nail kegs from out front and passed it over. "There you go," he said.

Jack sat down weakly on the keg and stared at the lunch before him. Andy divided everything in half: the brownie, the sandwich, and the four fried worms, giving Jack, naturally — his guest — the larger share.

"Okay, now, *big* bite," the photographer was saying, holding the camera up to his eye.

Andy lifted the grub sandwich to his lips. *Just pretend,* he told himself, *that you can either fall off the silo or take a bite of this sandwich.*

The bread moved even closer. Nothing would ever be so hard to swallow again — not even Aunt Wanda's Okra Surprise, Andy knew.

Crunch. His teeth bit into the roll and then the lettuce. Little chewy lumps of something settled on his tongue. Struggling not to gag, Andy swallowed as soon as he could.

"Yuk!" somebody said in the crowd.

Jack was still staring at his half of the sandwich.

Andy took another bite. Crunch again. The roll was fresh, the lettuce was crisp, and then he remembered what Sam had told him — that it doesn't matter what a food is called, or how it looks — it's how it *tastes* that matters.

Did he dare to actually taste the next bite? Did he dare to let his tongue search out the grubs in the mayonnaise?

"Looks delicious, doesn't it?" Mr. Sudermann was saying to the crowd. "When *this* boy says he'll dig up a little something for lunch, he means it!"

Everyone laughed.

Andy picked up one of the fried-worm bites. He thought of the delicious smell of the chicken in the Soul Food Kitchen and Carry-Out. Aunt Wanda's deep-fried batter smelled pretty good too. He put the worm in his mouth and swallowed without tasting. For a moment he thought it was stuck in his throat, just like in his dream — thought he might choke in front of the fifth-grade class. Then he felt it slide on down and reach his stomach at last. He took another bite and for just a moment let it linger. Was it possible . . . ? Yes, he was sure of it. Applesauce, just like the health inspector had said.

Jack was taking little nibbles of his sandwich from around the edge — grazing on the lettuce. He picked up a piece of fried worm and nibbled off a corner only, trying to usher it into his mouth by his teeth so that his lips wouldn't even touch it.

Well, he deserved it, Andy told himself, but all Jack had done, really, was giggle, and wouldn't Andy have done the same? He tried to think of the last really rotten thing Jack had done to him. Whatever it was, it had been a long time ago. Andy was good at holding grudges.

At that moment Sam reached out cautiously. "I'd like to try a bite of that sandwich, Andy," he said, and Andy knew he was only doing it to help.

"Why don't you eat Jack's?" he suggested, knowing that somehow, some way, he himself had to eat every bite of his own portion.

"*I* want to try something!" said Dora Kray's little brother who was too young to know better, and Jack shoved the fried worms toward him as though he couldn't give his food away fast enough.

"How about one more shot, now, of you two boys shaking hands?" the photographer said to Andy and Jack.

Jack was already standing, ready to run, and Andy stood up too and extended his hand, grinning at Jack.

Jack accepted it reluctantly.

"Pig face," he muttered as the camera clicked.

"Beetle breath," said Andy right back, but he smiled even more broadly.

Jack was smiling now in spite of himself.

"They're cousins," Mr. Sudermann was saying to the photographer. "Put that down in the photo caption." He smiled at the boys. "Maybe you fellas will grow up to be the next Wright brothers, who knows?"

15

Andy tried to imagine him and Jack inventing something together — actually spending time, dreaming up plans, seeing a project through. Somehow he imagined it very well.

"We might," he said, and walked back over to the pickup where Aunt Wanda stood waiting.

From
Anastasia Krupnik
by Lois Lowry

Anastasia uses her green notebook to sort out what's going on in her life. She keeps all kinds of lists there, too. This year, she's working on a new list: the most important things that happen to her the year she is ten.

Anastasia Krupnik was ten. She had hair the color of Hubbard squash, fourteen freckles across her nose (and seven others in places that she preferred people not to know about), and glasses with large owl-eyed rims, which she had chosen herself at the optician's.

Once she had thought that she might like to be a professional ice-skater. But after two years of trying, she still skated on the insides of her ankles.

Once she thought that she might like to be a ballerina, but after a year of Saturday morning ballet lessons, she still couldn't get the fifth position exactly right.

Her parents said, very kindly, that perhaps

she should choose a profession that didn't involve her feet. She thought that probably they were right, and she was still trying to think of one.

Anastasia had a small pink wart in the middle of her left thumb. She found her wart very pleasing. It had appeared quite by surprise, shortly after her tenth birthday, on a morning when nothing else interesting was happening, and it was the first wart she had ever had, or even seen.

"It's the loveliest color I've ever seen in a wart," her mother, who had seen others, said with admiration.

"Warts, you know," her father had told her, "have a kind of magic to them. They come and go without any reason at all, rather like elves."

Anastasia's father, Dr. Myron Krupnik, was a professor of literature and had read just about every book in the world, which may have been why he knew so much about warts. He had a beard the color of Hubbard squash, though not much hair on his head, and he wore glasses for astigmatism, as Anastasia did, although his were not quite as owly. He was also a poet. Sometimes he read his poems to Anastasia by candlelight, and let her take an occasional (very small) sip of his wine.

Katherine Krupnik, her mother, was a painter. Very often there was a smudge of purple on her cheek, or a daub of green on one wrist or elbow. Sometimes she smelled of turpentine, which painters use; sometimes she smelled of vanilla and brown sugar, which mothers use; and sometimes, not very often, she smelled of Je Reviens perfume.

In the bookcases of their apartment were four volumes of poetry, which had been written by Myron Krupnik. The first one was called *Laughter Behind the Mask,* and on the back of the book was a photograph of Myron Krupnik, much younger, when he had a lot of hair, holding his glass in one hand and half-smiling as if he knew a secret. Anastasia's father hated that book, or said that he did. Anastasia sometimes wondered why he kept it in the bookcase if he hated it so much. She thought it must be a little like the feeling she had had when she was eight, when she hated a boy named Michael McGuire so much that she walked past his house every day, just to stick out her tongue.

The second book of poetry by her father had a photograph of him with slightly less hair and a mustache; it was called *Mystery of Myth*. Her father liked it. But her mother didn't like it at all. The reason her mother didn't like it at all was because on one of the inside front pages it said, "For Annie." Anastasia didn't know who Annie was. She suspected that her mother did.

The third book was her mother's favorite, probably because *it* said, inside, "For Katherine." It was called *Come Morning, Come Night* and was filled with love poems that Anastasia found very embarrassing.

But the fourth book was her favorite. Her father's photograph showed him bald and bearded, the way she had always known him. The poems were soft-sounding and quiet, when he read them to her. The book was called *Bittersweet;* and it said, inside, "To someone special: Anastasia."

Sometimes, when no one was in the room, Anastasia took *Bittersweet* down from the shelf, just to look at that page. Looking at it made her feel awed, unique, and proud.

Awed, unique, and *proud* were three words that she had written on page seven of her green notebook. She kept lists of her favorite words; she kept important private information; and she kept things that she thought might be the beginnings of poems, in her green notebook. No one had ever looked inside the green notebook except Anastasia.

On page one, the green notebook said, "My name is Anastasia Krupnik. This is the year that I am ten."

On page two, it said, "These are the important things that happened the year that I was ten:"

So far, there were only two things on the list. One was, "I got a small pink wart." And the other was, "My teacher's name is Mrs. Westvessel."

Mrs. Westvessel wore stockings with seams up the back, and shoes that laced on the sides. Sometimes, while she sat at her desk, she unlaced her shoes when she thought no one was watching, and rubbed her feet against each other. Under the stockings, on the tops of her toes, were tiny round things like small doughnuts.

Anastasia described the toe doughnuts to her mother, and her mother nodded and explained that those were called corn pads.

Anastasia wrote "corn pads" on page twenty-seven of her notebook.

Mrs. Westvessel also had interesting brown spots on the backs of her hands, very large and lopsided bosoms, and a faint gray mustache.

"I think Mrs. Westvessel is probably over one hundred years old," Anastasia told her parents at dinner. "Probably about one hundred and twenty."

"Nobody lives to be one hundred and twenty," said her mother as she poured some mushroom gravy over Anastasia's meat loaf. "Unless they're in Tibet."

Her father wrinkled his forehead. "Perhaps Mrs. Westvessel is a mutant," he said.

"Yes," agreed Anastasia. "Mrs. Westvessel is a mutant, I believe."

Later she wrote "mutant" on page twenty-seven, under "corn pads." Anastasia was a very good speller; she sounded out the syllables of "mutant" correctly on the first try.

Anastasia didn't like Mrs. Westvessel very much. That made her feel funny, because she had always liked — sometimes even loved — her teachers before.

So she wrote in her green notebook, "Why don't I like Mrs. Westvessel?" and began to make a list of reasons. Making lists of reasons was sometimes a good way to figure things out.

"Reason one:" wrote Anastasia, "Because she isn't a good teacher."

But then she crossed out reason one, because it was a lie. Anastasia wasn't crazy about telling lies, even to herself; she did it, sometimes, but it always gave her a stomachache.

Mrs. Westvessel, she knew, was really a pretty good teacher. At any rate, she had taught Anastasia to remember the difference between minuends and subtrahends, which was not a particularly interesting thing to know; and also how to say "I love you" in both French and German, which was not only very interesting but might come in handy someday.

"Reason two:" wrote Anastasia, after she had crossed out reason *one,* "Because she is so old."

That wasn't a lie, so it didn't give her a stomachache; but it was a reason that Anastasia felt a little strange about. Anastasia felt a little strange about old people in general. Probably it was because of her grandmother, who was the oldest person she knew. Her grandmother was so old that she lived in a nursing home, and Anastasia didn't like to visit her there. The nursing home smelled of medicine and Polident, a bad combination of smells.

But Mrs. Westvessel smelled of chalk dust

and Elmer's Glue, which was not a bad combination at all. And Mrs. Westvessel, although
she was old, never *acted* old. When they were
studying Ireland in geography, Mrs. Westvessel had done an Irish jig in her laced-up shoes,
with her bosoms bouncing. *That,* thought
Anastasia, wasn't an *old* thing to do.

So she slowly crossed out reason *two.*
Then she couldn't think of any others.

Finally she wrote, *"Reason three:* Because
I am dumb."

Not dumb in school. Anastasia, particularly after she had finally mastered the difference between minuends and subtrahends,
was actually a very good student.

"I'm dumb," said Anastasia sadly to herself,
"because sometimes — too many times — I
don't feel the same way about things that
everybody else feels.

"I was the only one at Jennifer Mac-
Cauley's birthday party," she remembered
gloomily, "who thought green ice cream was
nauseating. Everybody even *said* I was dumb
for that.

"I'm the only person in the world," she reminded herself, "— the whole entire world —
who likes cold spinach sandwiches. That's
really dumb.

"And now," she thought, "I'm the only kid

in the fourth grade who doesn't like Mrs. Westvessel."

So reason *three* seemed to be the reason. "Because I'm dumb." She left it there, frowned, and closed her green notebook. "Sometimes," she thought, "maybe it isn't a good idea after all to make a list and find out the answer to a question."

But when Mrs. Westvessel announced one day in the fall that the class would begin writing poetry, Anastasia was the happiest she had ever been in school.

Somewhere, off in a place beyond her own thoughts, Anastasia could hear Mrs.Westvessel's voice. She was reading some poems to the class; she was talking about poetry and how it was made. But Anastasia wasn't really listening. She was listening instead to the words that were appearing in her own head, floating there and arranging themselves into groups, into lines, into poems.

There were so many poems being born in Anastasia's head that she ran all the way home from school to find a private place to write them down, the way her cat had once found a very private place — the pile of ironing in the pantry — in which to create kittens.

But she discovered that it wasn't easy. She

hung the DO NOT DISTURB sign from the Parker House Hotel on the doorknob of her bedroom door. She thought that might make it easier.

She got herself a glass of orange juice with ice in it, to sip on while she worked. She thought that might make it easier.

She put on her Red Sox cap. She thought that might make it easier.

But it still wasn't easy at all. Sometimes the words she wrote down were the wrong words, and didn't say what she wanted them to say, didn't make the sounds that she wanted them to make. Soon her Snoopy wastebasket was filled with crumpled pages, crumpled beginnings of poems.

Her mother knocked on her bedroom door and called, "Anastasia? Are you all right?"

"Yes," she called back, taking her pencil eraser out of her mouth for a minute. "I'm writing a poem."

Her mother understood that, because very often Anastasia's father would close the door to his study when he was writing a poem, and wouldn't come out even for dinner. "Okay, love," her mother said, the way she said it to Anastasia's father.

It took her eight evenings to write one poem. Even then, she was surprised when she realized that it was finished. She read it aloud, alone in her room, behind the DO NOT DISTURB sign from the Parker House Hotel; and then she read it aloud again, and smiled.

Then she read it aloud one more time, put it into the top drawer of her desk, took out her green notebook, and added to the list on page two under "These are the most important things that happened the year that I was ten," as item three: "I wrote a wonderful poem."

Then she flipped the DO NOT DISTURB sign on her doorknob to its opposite side, the side her mother didn't like. "Maid," said the opposite side, "please make up this room as soon as possible."

Her poem was finished just in time for Creativity Week.

Mrs. Westvessel was very, very fond of Weeks. In their class, already this year, they had had Be Kind to Animals Week, when the bulletin board had been filled with newspaper clippings about dogs that had found lost children in deep woods, cats that had traveled three hundred miles home after being left behind in strange cities, and a cow in New Hampshire that had been spray-painted red during hunting season so that she would not be mistaken for a deer.

During My Neighborhood Week, one entire classroom wall had been covered with paper on which they had made a mural: each child had drawn a building to create My Neighborhood. There were three Luigi's Pizzas; two movie theaters, both showing *Superman;* one Red Sox Stadium; a split-level house with a horse tied to a tree in the yard; two Aquariums; two Science Museums; one Airport control tower; three State Prisons; and a condemned apartment building with a large rat on the front steps. Mrs. Westvessel said that it was not what she had had in mind, and that next time she would give better instructions.

Creativity Week was the week that the fourth grade was to bring their poems to school. On Monday morning Mrs. Westvessel took them on a field trip to Longfellow's home on Brattle Street. On Tuesday afternoon, a lady poet — poetess, she should be called, according to Mrs. Westvessel; but the lady poet frowned and said she preferred poet, please — came to visit the class and read some of her poems. The lady poet wore dark glasses and had crimson fingernails. Anastasia didn't think that Longfellow would have liked the lady poet at all, *or* her poems.

Wednesday was the day that the members

of the class were to read their own poems, aloud.

Robert Giannini stood in front of the class and read:

> *I have a dog whose name is Spot.*
> *He likes to eat and drink a lot.*
> *When I put water in his dish,*
> *He laps it up just like a fish.*

Anastasia hated Robert Giannini's poem. Also, she thought it was a lie. Robert Giannini's dog was named Sputnik; everyone in the neighborhood knew that; and Sputnik had bitten two kids during the summer and if he bit one more person the police said the Gianninis would have to get rid of him.

But Mrs. Westvessel cried, "Wonderful!" She gave Robert Giannini an A and hung his poem on the wall. Anastasia imagined that Longfellow was eyeing it with distaste.

Traci Beckwith got up from her desk, straightened her tights carefully, and read:

> *In autumn when the trees are brown,*
> *I like to walk all through the town.*
> *I like to see the birds fly south.*
> *Some have worms, still, in their mouths.*

Traci Beckwith blushed, and said, "It doesn't rhyme exactly."

"Well," said Mrs. Westvessel, in a kind voice, "your next one will be better, I'm sure." She gave Traci Beckwith a B plus, and hung the poem on the wall next to Robert's.

Anastasia had begun to feel a little funny, as if she had ginger ale inside of her knees. But it was her turn. She stood up in front of the class and read her poem. Her voice was very small, because she was nervous.

hush   hush   the sea-soft night is aswim
with wrinklesquirm creatures
                    listen (!)
to them   move   smooth   in the moistly dark
here in the   whisperwarm   wet

That was Anastasia's poem.

"Read that again, please, Anastasia, in a bigger voice," said Mrs. Westvessel.

So Anastasia took a deep breath and read her poem again. She used the same kind of voice that her father did when he read poetry to her, drawing some of the words out as long as licorice sticks, and making some others thumpingly short.

The class laughed.

30

Mrs. Westvessel looked puzzled. "Let me see that, Anastasia," she said. Anastasia gave her the poem.

Mrs. Westvessel's ordinary, everyday face had about one hundred wrinkles in it. When she looked at Anastasia's poem, her forehead and nose folded up so that she had two hundred new wrinkles all of a sudden.

"Where are your capital letters, Anastasia?" asked Mrs. Westvessel.

Anastasia didn't say anything.

"Where is the rhyme?" asked Mrs. Westvessel. "It doesn't rhyme at *all*."

Anastasia didn't say anything.

"What kind of poem *is* this, Anastasia?" asked Mrs. Westvessel. "Can you explain it, please?"

Anastasia's voice had become very small again, the way voices do, sometimes. "It's a poem of sounds," she said. "It's about little things that live in tidepools, after dark, when they move around. It doesn't have sentences or capital letters because I wanted it to look on the page like small creatures moving in the dark."

"I don't know why it doesn't rhyme," she said miserably. "It didn't seem important."

"Anastasia, weren't you *listening* in class when we talked about writing poems?"

Anastasia looked at the floor. "No," she whispered, finally.

Mrs. Westvessel frowned, and rubbed her jiggly bosoms thoughtfully. "Well," she said, at last.

"Well. Anastasia, when we talked about poetry in this class we simply were not talking about worms and snails crawling on a piece of paper. I'm afraid I will have to give you an F."

An F. Anastasia had never had an F in her entire life. She kept looking at the floor. Someone had stepped on a red crayon once; the color was smeared into the wood forever.

"Iworkedveryhardonthatpoem," whispered Anastasia to the floor.

"Speak up, Anastasia."

Anastasia lifted her head and looked Mrs. Westvessel in the eye. "I worked very, very hard on that poem," she said, in a loud, clear voice.

Mrs. Westvessel looked terribly sad. "I can tell that you did, Anastasia," she said. "But the trouble is that you didn't listen to the instructions. I gave very, very careful instructions to the class about the kind of poems you were to write. And you were here that day; I remember that you were.

"Now if, in geography, I explained to the class just how to draw a map, and someone didn't listen, and drew his own kind of map" (everyone glanced at Robert Giannini, who blushed — he had drawn a beautiful map of Ireland, with cartoon figures of people throwing bombs all over it, and had gotten an F) "even though it was a very *beautiful* map, I would have to give that person a failing grade because he didn't follow the instructions. So I'm afraid I will have to do the same in this case, Anastasia.

"I'm sorry," said Mrs. Westvessel.

"I just bet you are," thought Anastasia.

"If you work hard on another, perhaps it will be better. I'm *sure* it will be better," said Mrs. Westvessel. She wrote a large F on the page of poetry, gave it back to Anastasia, and called on the next student.

At home, that evening, Anastasia got her green notebook out of her desk drawer. Solemnly, under "These are the most important things that happened the year that I was ten," in item three, she crossed out the word *wonderful* and replaced it with the word *terrible*.

"I wrote a terrible poem," she read sadly. Her goldfish, Frank, came to the side of his bowl and moved his mouth. Anastasia read his lips and said, "Blurp blurp blurp to you too, Frank."

Then she turned the pages of her notebook until she came to a blank one, page fourteen, and printed carefully at the top of the right-hand side: THINGS I HATE.

She thought very hard because she wanted it to be an honest list.

Finally she wrote down: "Mr. Belden at the drugstore." Anastasia honestly hated Mr. Belden, because he called her "girlie," and because once, in front of a whole group of fifth-grade boys who were buying baseball cards, he had said the rottenest, rudest thing she could imagine anyone saying ever, and especially in front of a whole group of fifth-grade boys. Mr. Belden had said, "You want some Kover-up Kreme for those freckles, girlie?" And she had not been anywhere *near* the Kover-up Freckle Kreme, which was $1.39 and right between the Cuticura Soap and the Absorbine Jr.

Next, without any hesitation, Anastasia wrote down "Boys." She honestly hated boys. All of the fifth-grade boys buying baseball cards that day had laughed.

"Liver" was also an honest thing. Everybody in the world hated liver except her parents.

34

And she wrote down "pumpkin pie," after some thought. She had *tried* to like pumpkin pie, but she honestly hated it.

And finally, Anastasia wrote, at the end of her THINGS I HATE list: "Mrs. Westvessel." That was the most honest thing of all.

Then, to even off the page, she made a list on the left-hand side: THINGS I LOVE. For some reason it was an easier list to make.

Her parents were having coffee in the living room. "They're going to find out about the F when they go for a parent-teacher conference," thought Anastasia. "So I might as well show them." She took her poem to the living room. She held it casually behind her back.

"You guys know," she said, "how sometimes maybe someone is a great musician or something — well, maybe he plays the trumpet or something really well — and then maybe he has a kid, and it turns out the kid isn't any good at *all* at playing the trumpet?" Her parents looked puzzled.

"No," said her father. "What on earth are you talking about?"

She tried again. "Well, suppose a guy is a terrific basketball player. Maybe he plays for the Celtics and he's almost seven feet tall. Then maybe he has a kid, a little boy, and maybe the little boy *wants* to be a great basketball player. But he only grows to be five feet tall. So he can't be any good at basketball, right?"

"Is it a riddle, Anastasia?" her mother asked. "It seems very complicated."

"What if a man is a really good poet and his daughter tries to write a poem — I mean tries *really hard* — and the only poem she writes is a *terrible* poem?"

"Oh," said her father. "Let's see the poem, Anastasia."

Anastasia handed the poem to her father.

He read it once to himself. Then he read it aloud. He read it the way Anastasia had tried to, in class, so that some of the words sounded long and shuddery. When he came to the word "night" he said it in a voice as quiet as sleep. When he had finished, they were all silent for a moment. Her parents looked at each other.

"You know, Anastasia," her father said, finally. "Some people — actually, a *lot* of people — just don't understand poetry."

"It doesn't make them bad people," said her mother hastily.

"Just *dumb*?" suggested Anastasia. If she could change, under "Why don't I like Mrs. Westvessel?" the answer "Because I'm dumb" to "Because *she's* dumb," maybe it wouldn't be such a discouraging question and answer after all.

But her father disagreed. "Not dumb," he said. "Maybe they just haven't been educated to understand poetry."

He took his red pen from his pocket. "I myself," he said grandly, "have been *very* well educated to understand poetry." With his red pen he added some letters to the F, so that the word *Fabulous* appeared across the top of the page.

Anastasia decided that when she went back to her room she would get her green notebook out again, and change page two once more. "I wrote a fabulous poem," it would say. She smiled.

"Daddy, do you think maybe someday I could be a poet?" she asked.

"Don't know why not," he said. "If you work hard at it."

"How long does it take to make a whole book of poems?"

"Well, let's see. That last book of mine took me about nine months."

Anastasia groaned. "That's a long time. You could get a *baby* in nine months, for pete's sake."

Her parents both laughed. Then they

looked at each other and laughed harder. Suddenly Anastasia had a very strange feeling that she knew why they were laughing. She had a very strange feeling that her list of things THINGS I HATE was going to be getting even longer.

From
Everyone Else's Parents Said Yes
by Paula Danziger

In his sixth-grade class at Elizabeth Englebert Elementary (or E.E.E., where the cheer "go E.E.E." sounds like pigs squealing), Matthew Martin is the youngest kid of all. Everyone else is eleven, but not Matthew. He's really looking forward to his birthday, but first he's going to have to deal with the declaration of war that landed on his desk this morning.

We, the girls of Grade Six of E.E.E., do hereby form an organization called GET HIM, which is short for Girls Eager to Halt Immature Matthew.

We plan to do everything possible to make Matthew Martin's life as miserable as he has made ours.

SO, MATTHEW MARTIN, WATCH OUT!!!!!!!

THE GET HIM EXPLANATION:

Just so people don't think that we are being unfair ganging up on Matthew Martin, fink of Califon, fink of New Jersey, fink of the United States. North America. Earth. The Universe. Matthew Martin, slimeball of all eternity, we do hereby list just a few of the sneaky, disgusting, and rotten things that he has done to us!

1. Putting catsup and mayonnaise in his mouth, puffing up his cheeks, smacking them to make the goop come out of his face onto Cathy Atwood's brand-new dress, and screaming, "I'm a zit! I'm a zit!"

2. Always making fun of Jessica Weeks's last name, saying dumb things like "Jessica Weeks makes many daze." And whenever he sees her with her parents and little sister, yelling out, "Look! It's the Month family — Four Weeks equals one month." Enough is enough!

3. Rolling up rubber cement into tiny balls, labeling them "snot balls," and putting them into Lisa Levine's pencil box.

4. Ever since preschool, kicking the bottom of the chair of the person who is unlucky enough to be seated in front of him.

5. Whenever anyone taller stands up in front of him, yelling, "I can't see through you. What do you think, that your father's a glazier?" We can't help it if practically everyone in the class is taller than Matthew. It's especially mean when he does it to Katie Delaney. She can't help it if she's the tallest person in the class.

6. Putting a "Sushi for Sale" sign in the class aquarium.

7. Teasing any boy who wants to talk to one of the girls, acting as if it were the crime of the century. Just wait until Matthew gets old enough and acts more mature (if that ever happens, especially since he is the baby of the class) and wants to ask some girl out on a date. No one in this class is ever ever going to go out with him. We've made a solemn promise as part of GET HIM. He's going to have to ask out some girl who is presently in preschool or not even born yet because we have also made a solemn promise

to inform every girl in the world to WATCH OUT!

8. During the Spring Concert quietly singing the theme song from that ancient TV show *Mr. Ed* while everyone else was trying to sing the correct songs.

9. Putting Bubble Yum in Zoe Alexander's very very long blond hair, so that her mother had to spend four hours rubbing ice cubes on it, and then, when told about what a pain it was, said, "I guess that helped you cool off, you hothead."

10. On last year's class trip to the Bronx Zoo, going up to the attendants, pointing to all the girls, and saying that they had escaped from the monkey cages.

11. Bothering all the girls at lunchtime to make them trade their meals for the sprouty stuff he always brings.

12. Always acting like such a big shot about computer stuff, never helping out any girl who needs help, and acting like Chloe Fulton doesn't exist because she's almost as

good as he is at it and could be even better if she didn't have so many other interests. SO THERE!

13. For the Valentine Box, giving the girls envelopes filled with night crawlers. Even though it was anonymous, we all know who did it. Even if Mrs. Stanton said we couldn't prove it, we know it was Matthew because most of the names were spelled wrong. So was the handwritten message, LET ME WERM MY WAY INTO YOUR HART.

We, the eleven members of GET HIM, could go on forever listing all the stuff he's done to us, but we've decided to list just thirteen things. The unlucky number, thirteen, is only the beginning.

From now on Matthew Martin is going to have to watch out. We're going to make his life as miserable as he has made ours. He's never going to know when something is going to happen.

WE ARE SERIOUS!!!!!!!!!!!!!!!!!!!!!!!!!!!!!!!!!!
WE ARE ANGRY!!!!!!!!!!!!!!!!!!!!!!!!!!!!!!!!!!!!
WE AREN'T GOING TO TAKE IT ANY-MORE!!!!!!!!!!!!!!!!!!!!!!!!!!

SIGNED,

VANESSA SINGER, President

KATIE DELANEY, Vice President

JIL! HUDSON, Secretary

LIZZIE DORAN, Treasurer

MEMBERS: Cathy Atwood, Lisa Levine, Jessica Weeks, Zoe Alexander, Chloe Fulton, Ryma Browne, and Sarah Montgomery

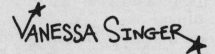

44

Lizzie Doran

Cathy Atwood   Lisa Levine

Sarah Montgomery   Jessica Weeks

Ayma Browne

Zoe Alexander

"You're in for it," Joshua says, when the boys discover the GET HIM declaration on Matthew's desk. "I'm glad that I'm not you."

"Me too," says Tyler White. "But then I'm always glad that I'm not you. I'm glad I'm not you when we're playing Keepaway. I'm glad I'm not you when we're opening up our lunches. I'm glad —"

"Shut up," Matthew says.

Tyler continues, "And I'm really glad that I'm not you today. When all the girls gang up on someone, it's awful."

Matthew looks at the declaration that has been stuck to his desk with plastic imitation dog doo and then he looks up at Tyler again. "Shut up."

"Really original." Tyler smiles at him.

"You only wish you were me when we're playing with the computer or Nintendo." Matthew stares at him.

Tyler stares back, but he's the first one to blink and look away.

Matthew smiles for the first time since he's gotten into the classroom and seen what's on his desk.

All of the boys in the class are crowding around his desk.

All of the girls are standing by the aquarium, talking to each other and looking his way.

Some of the girls are giggling.

Others are glaring.

Vanessa Singer looks very proud of herself.

Matthew looks around the classroom and tries to figure out what to do next.

The girls keep glaring and giggling.

Matthew is in deep trouble and he knows it.

He's not going to let anyone else know that he knows it.

Mrs. Stanton walks into the room and looks around.

Everyone tries to look very innocent. They immediately head for their desks, very quietly.

Mrs. Stanton looks around, trying to figure out what's going on without making too big a deal of it.

She looks at Matthew, who she figures has probably done something.

He is putting away the incriminating evidence, the plastic dog doo and the declaration.

It's going right into his backpack.

There's no way that he's going to be a squealer.

That just isn't done in the sixth grade at E.E.E.

It's okay to tell on a brother or sister at home but not to tell on a classmate at school, as long as it's not a serious thing, the kind of thing that kids really should tell grown-ups.

This is not a serious thing. It's serious, but not SERIOUS, like drugs or abuse or something dangerous.

There's no way that he's going to act like a baby and have Mrs. Stanton take care of it by talking to the girls. That would only make things worse, and Matthew Martin has a feeling that things are going to be bad enough as it is.

Vanessa Singer keeps sneaking looks at him and snickering.

"Would you like to share the joke with us, Vanessa, dear?" Mrs. Stanton says stuff like that a lot when she wants kids to stop fooling around.

It works.

Vanessa takes her notebook out of her desk and looks at the next spelling list.

So does everyone else.

There is a lot of giggling going around.

Not just the girls, but the boys too.

All of the boys but Matthew, who is beginning to wonder if he's finally going to be paid back for all the things he has done to other people.

Matthew goes into his desk and takes out his spelling list.

Someone has put Saran Wrap over all the stuff in his desk and covered the wrap with lime Jell-O. It keeps wiggling back and forth.

It looks so gross.

Matthew wishes he had thought of doing it . . . to someone else, probably to Vanessa Singer. But he would have added little pieces of his mother's tofu, which would have made it look really gross.

But he didn't think of it. Someone else did and now it was in Matthew's desk, looking like the Slime That Ate Califon.

Green Jell-O was the only flavor he hated. Someone who knew his habits was out to get him.

Looking around the room, he realized that there were eleven someones who were out to get him.

This wasn't fair to do to someone with a birthday coming up, someone who was going to be very busy getting ready for his party, someone who didn't want to waste his time thinking about what a bunch of dumb girls were going to do to him.

Maybe this will be it, Matthew thinks. Maybe the dumb girls have had their dumb fun and they'll leave me alone.

Three minutes later Matthew feels someone kicking the bottom of his chair.

He turns around to check it out.

It's Lizzie Doran . . . and she's smiling.

From
Bud, Not Buddy
by Christopher Paul Curtis

This Newbery Award–winner tells the story of Bud Caldwell, a motherless boy on the run in 1936. Bud has just escaped from the Amoses' wretched foster home. Fortunately, he hasn't lost his sense of humor, or his suitcase filled with all of his important stuff. Unfortunately, he's not exactly sure what his next step should be. But he's positive of one thing: Deciding is definitely up to him, and him alone.

Being on the lam was a whole lot of fun . . . for about five minutes. Every time my heart beat I could feel the blood pushing hot and hard on the inside of my sting spots and the bite on my hand. But I couldn't let that slow me down, I had to get out of this neighborhood as quick as I could.

I knew a nervous-looking, stung-up kid with blood dripping from a fish-head bite and carrying a old raggedy suitcase didn't look like he belonged around here.

The only hope I had was the north side library. If I got there, maybe Miss Hill would be able to help me, maybe she'd understand and would be able to tell me what to do. And for now I could sneak into the library's basement to sleep.

It was a lot later than I'd ever been up before and I was kind of scared of the cops catching me. I had to be real careful, even if it was the middle of the night, even if I was crouching down, sneaking along the street like Pretty Boy Floyd.

At the library I walked past a row of giant Christmas trees that were planted on the side of the building. There was a door on the side with a light burning above it, so I kept walking in the shadows made by the big trees. When I got to the back windows, I almost busted out crying. Somebody had gone and put big metal bars on the windows.

Even though I knew it was useless I tried tugging at the bars but they were the real McCoy, solid steel.

I headed back to the Christmas trees. They were low enough to the ground that no one could see me unless they were really looking, so I started opening my suitcase. Most folks don't have sense enough to carry a blanket around with them, but you never know when you might be sleeping under a Christmas tree at the library so I always keep mine handy.

I untied the strange knots that the Amoses had put in my twine and opened the suitcase. I could tell right away that someone had been fumbling through my things. First off, whenever I put the blanket in, I always fold it so that it stops all the other things from banging up against each other, but those doggone Amoses had just stuffed it in without paying no mind to what it was mashing up against.

I lifted the blanket out and saw that everything else was still there. You might be able to say that the Amoses were some mean old nosy folks, but you couldn't call them thieves.

I picked up the old tobacco bag that I keep my rocks in. I could tell by the way the drawstring was pulled that the Amoses had been poking through this too. I jiggled it up and down in my hand a couple of times and it felt like none of the rocks was missing but I opened it to count them anyway. None of them was gone.

Next I pulled Momma's picture out of the envelope I kept it in and held it so the light from the library's side door would shine down on it.

It looked like the Amoses hadn't hurt it. This was the only picture of Momma in the world. Running acrost the top of it was a sign that was writ on a long skinny flag, it said, BOYS AND GIRLS — FOLLOW THE GENTLE LIGHT TO THE MISS B. GOTTEN MOON PARK. Underneath the sign, between the two big wagon wheels, was Momma.

She was about as old as I am now and was looking down and frowning. I can't understand why she was so unhappy, this park looked like the kind of place where you could have a lot of fun.

In the picture Momma was sitting on a real live little midget horse. It looked tired and dragged out like those big workhorses do, but it had a teeny-tiny body with a big sag where most horses have a straight back.

Momma was sitting right in the middle of the horse's back, riding him sidesaddle, except there wasn't any saddle so I guess you have to say she was riding him side-sag. She had two six-shooter pistols in her hands and the way her face looked you could tell she wished she could've emptied them on somebody. And I know who that somebody was. Momma told me it was her father, my granddad.

He'd gone and ruined everybody's fun that day by getting in a big fight with my mother about the gigantic white twenty-five-gallon Texas cowboy hat that she was wearing.

Momma used to tell me, "That hard-headed man insisted, insisted mind you, that I wear that horrible hat."

The hat was almost as big as Momma and you could see it was fake because as tall as it was no real cowboy could've wore it without getting it knocked off his head every time he rode under a tree or some telegraph wires.

Momma told me that some man used to drag the midget horse all through her neighborhood with a camera and if your momma or daddy signed a piece of paper he'd take some pictures of you, then come back in a couple of weeks so you could buy them. Momma wasn't looking like she had rocks in her jaw because the hat was so fake that a real cowboy would've laughed you out of town for wearing it, she was mad because the hat was so dirty.

When she used to tell me about it, her eyes would get big and burny, like the whole thing happened the day before yesterday instead of all those years ago. She'd start moving around our apartment real quick, picking things up and putting them back in the exact same spot.

"Filth!" she'd say about the hat. "Absolute

filth! Why, the thing was positively alive with germs! Who knows what type of people had worn it?"

I'd say, "I don't know, Momma."

She'd say, "Who knows how many years it had been worn by who knows how many sweaty little heads?"

I'd say, "I don't know, Momma."

She'd say, "The entire band on the inside was black and I'm sure it was crawling with ringworm, lice, and tetters!"

I'd say, "Yes, Momma."

She'd say, "And that horrid little photographer didn't care, do you imagine it ever occurred to him to wash it?"

I'd say, "No, Momma."

She'd say, "Of course not, we meant less to him than that horse he mistreated so."

I'd say, "Yes, Momma."

She'd say, "But your grandfather insisted. To this day I cannot understand why, but he insisted, insisted . . ."

I'd say, "Yes, Momma."

We had that conversation a lot of times.

Me and Momma having the same conversations lots of times is one of the main things I can remember about her now. Maybe that's because when she'd tell me these things she used to squeeze my arms and look right hard in my face to make sure I was listening, but maybe I remember them because those arm-squeezing, face-looking times were the only times that things slowed down a little bit when Momma was around.

Everything moved very, very fast when Momma was near, she was like a tornado, never resting, always looking around us, never standing still. The only time stuff didn't blow around when she was near was when she'd squeeze my arms and tell me things over and over and over and over.

She had four favorite things to tell me, one of them was about the picture and another one was about my name.

She'd say, "Bud is your name and don't you ever let anyone call you anything outside of that either."

She'd tell me, "Especially don't you ever let anyone call you Buddy, I may have some problems but being stupid isn't one of them, I would've added that *dy* onto the end of your name if I intended for it to be there. I knew what I was doing, Buddy is a dog's name or a name that someone's going to use on you if they're being false-friendly. Your name is Bud, period."

I'd say, "OK, Momma."

And she'd say, every single time, "And do you know what a bud is?"

I always answered, "Yes, Momma," but it was like she didn't hear me, she'd tell me anyway.

"A bud is a flower-to-be. A flower-in-waiting. Waiting for just the right warmth and care to open up. It's a little fist of love waiting to unfold and be seen by the world. And that's you."

I'd say, "Yes, Momma."

I know she didn't mean anything by naming me after a flower, but it's sure not something I tell anybody about.

Another thing she'd tell me was, "Don't you worry, Bud, as soon as you get to be a young man I have a lot of things I'll explain to you." That didn't make me calm at all, that was Bud Caldwell's Rules and Things to Have a Funner Life and Make a Better Liar Out of Yourself Number 83.

RULES AND THINGS NUMBER 83

If a Adult Tells You Not to Worry,
and You Weren't Worried Before,
You Better Hurry Up
and Start 'Cause You're Already
Running Late.

She'd tell me, "These things I'm going to explain to you later will be a great help for you." Then Momma'd look hard in my face, grab a holt of my arms real tight, and say, "And Bud, I want you always to remember, no matter how bad things look to you, no matter how dark the night, when one door closes, don't worry, because another door opens."

I'd say, "What, it opens all by itself?"

She'd say, "Yes, it seems so."

That was it: "Another door opens." That was the thing that was supposed to have helped me. I should've known then that I was in for a lot of trouble.

It's funny how now that I'm ten years old and just about a man I can see how Momma was so wrong. She was wrong because she probably should've told me the things she thought I was too young to hear, because now that she's gone I'll never know what they were. Even if I was too young back then I could've rememorized them and used them when I did need help, like right now.

She was also wrong when she thought I'd understand that nonsense about doors closing and opening all by themselves. Back then it really scared me because I couldn't see what one door closing had to do with another one opening unless there was a ghost involved. All her talk made me start jamming a chair up against my closet door at night.

But now that I'm almost grown I see Momma wasn't talking about doors opening to let ghosts into your bedroom, she meant doors like the door at the Home closing leading to the door at the Amoses' opening and the door in the shed opening leading to me sleeping under a tree getting ready to open the next door.

I checked out the other things in my suitcase and they seemed OK. I felt a lot better.

Right now I was too tired to think anymore so I closed my suitcase, put the proper knots back in the twine, crawled under the Christmas tree, and wrapped myself in the blanket.

From
Yolonda's Genius
by Carol Fenner

*In this Newbery Honor Book, Yolonda and her
family have moved away from Chicago because things were too dangerous there. But it's
not that easy in their new suburban home, either. Yolonda misses her old friend Tyrone, and
she worries about her little brother, Andrew.
He's quiet and communicates mostly through
music. Yolonda looks out for him — especially
since she's the only one who sees how gifted he
is. Now Andrew's harmonica is broken, and
Yolonda can't understand what happened.*

Why would a musical genius break his harmonica? Yolonda puzzled about this over
and over. One of Andrew's teachers had even
stopped Yolanda in the hallway at school.
"Wh-what's the d-deal with Andrew's harmonica? The b-boy won't say."

Yolonda had just shrugged, her protective
instincts flaring. Who was this guy anyway?
"He has a flute at home," she had said, not

lying — not telling the truth. There had been no waking-up music in the morning for days — ever since the harmonica-in-the-tulip-bed incident. Not a sound came from Andrew's little pipe.

Aunt Tiny had given Andrew the pipe when she started Yolonda on piano lessons. At first Yolonda thought maybe Andrew had broken his pipe, too. Maybe wrecking his harmonica was some kind of creative fit geniuses went into. Van Gogh painted ordinary things so that you could see them in waves of rippling color; he cut off his own ear in a rage of frustration, then painted a self-portrait with a bandaged head. She'd also heard of writers ripping up manuscripts they were unhappy with. But Andrew didn't get frustrated. He never judged his music. He just played it. One thing Yolonda knew: Andrew needed his harmonica. He wasn't the same Andrew without it.

"I don't think that's wise, Yolonda," her mother said one morning when Yolonda asked her for money to replace Andrew's harmonica. Yolonda was helping with breakfast partly because her momma had an early meeting to attend but mostly because Yolonda wanted money.

"If he's been that careless with a good in-strument," continued her momma, "then he's not responsible enough yet to have another one." She whisked an egg into the buttermilk for pancakes. "Maybe it's a sign he's growing up. Miss Gilluly at the school has been dis-turbed by his hanging on to that old harp like it was a 'blankie' to suck his thumb with."

"Andrew never sucks his thumb," protested Yolonda.

"That's not the issue, Yolonda Mae." Her momma always stuck the *Mae* in there like a steel exclamation point when she wanted no argument. "The issue is that his harmonica has interfered with his concentration on schoolwork. Now turn on the griddle, please."

"Yeah, but Momma . . . ," stalled Yolonda.

"Discussion ended," said her mother, whipping off her apron.

Yolonda searched her brain for a way to tell her mother about Andrew being a genius, but her mother was in such a hurry. Yolonda couldn't get into the stuff about true genius rearranging old material. So she just got right to the point.

"Andrew's a genius, Mother." She used her teacher voice, serious and deliberate. "He's a musical genius. He needs gifted teachers who know how to teach geniuses. He ought to be studying horn or some other wind instrument. Did you ever listen to the way —"

"Have you turned on the griddle, miss?" Her mother was getting out plates. "Andrew is Andrew," she said. "He's a *normal* child." Yolonda thought she heard a flash of panic in her mother's voice. But maybe she imagined it. The panic flickered away as quickly as it had appeared. Her momma's voice was soft now. "Andrew is Andrew. That means a little boy, a pretty little boy. Your daddy's face must have looked like that when he was little. Eyes the color of chestnuts, Andrew is going to grow up to look like his daddy. He'll probably be a police officer like his father." Mrs. Blue paused, smiling. "Yolonda, remember your daddy — how fine he looked in his uniform? Tall, that broad chest? Remember? He always smelled so good."

But Yolonda was shocked into silence. A police officer? Andrew a cop? She was aghast. Before she could even get a proper protest or a sarcastic laugh out of her mouth, her mother was jerking into her coat. "Set the table right, Yolonda." Grabbing her briefcase. "Make sure Andrew eats." The door slammed.

Yolonda did remember her father's size. Andrew's fine looks and small-boned body were more like her momma's. *She* was her daddy's child, large and strong.

"The only one in this family suited to police work," she told her absent mother loudly, "is yours truly, Yolonda Mae!"

She tested the griddle with a sprinkle of cold water. It gave a satisfying hiss, a signal that usually made her mouth juice up. The weight of Andrew's genius forced her breath out in a huge sigh. Today, she didn't even want her own breakfast, much less part of her brother's. She heard his soft step coming into the kitchen and she had a painful image of Andrew's extraordinary spirit sickening — all that new way of hearing ordinary old stuff growing dim. The guilt over neglecting Andrew while she baked a cake with Shirley surfaced in a rush and bit her. What could she do to take it back — to bring Andrew back?

First Yolonda had considered raiding Andrew's bank. After all, the harmonica was for him. Andrew got three dollars a week, which Yolonda changed into quarters for him. He dropped them, clink by lovely clink, into the slot of his giant panda bank. The bank had no other opening. Yolonda estimated Andrew had over a hundred and fifty dollars in quarters in that giant panda.

In the end Yolonda raided her own savings box and took eight dollars in bills and change. She thought she remembered her daddy saying you could get a top-grade mouth harp for about five dollars and Yolonda was allowing for inflation.

They probably don't even make the Marine Band harmonica anymore, she thought. But she'd look.

Her momma had said "no harmonica." But the stone-dead look of Andrew's face had been haunting Yolonda. She hadn't been able to get it through her momma's head about Andrew being a genius. Her momma wouldn't listen; served her right if her daughter didn't obey.

She waited for the bus to the big mall, her hand jammed against the money in her jeans pocket. They might just as well have stayed in Chicago where she knew how to take care of Andrew and herself, where she didn't need any friends. Where there was a bus every five minutes.

This bus took so long coming that she almost went home twice — walked halfway down the block. She almost never directly disobeyed her mother. She argued with her instead. She could hardly stand the feeling of being sneaky.

But the bus came and she climbed on, keeping Andrew's deadened face in her mind. Then it came to her in a flash who his stone-dead expression reminded her of. As she sat, her hands cramped and sweating around the crumpled dollar bills and quarters in her pocket, another face exchanged itself for Andrew's. Tyrone's!

She saw his eyes, their brightness gone. She saw the drooping mouth where once a sassy smile had caught her heart.

"Tyrone," she gasped aloud. Dragging through her memory was the image of his shrunken figure led away between two police officers. *Tyrone.*

What kind of prison was Andrew in? Yolonda felt her resolve strengthen. She would bring Andrew back.

The big mall had a lot of stores, both indoors and outside. It was Saturday and the whole area was filled with real shoppers and window-shoppers and teenage kids in clusters.

The harmonica in Kresge's was small — only four holes. It cost $2.98 and appeared to be fragile. Besides, it wasn't covered with plastic or anything. Any yo-yo could pick it up and slobber all over it. Andrew didn't need anybody's germs, and this harmonica didn't look like it would withstand boiling water.

Next she checked Toy Paradise, marching down aisles and aisles of towering warehouse shelves filled with toys.

"Harmonicas?" Yolonda punched out the question at a dazed-looking salesclerk. The girl, who didn't look much older than Yolonda, suggested aisle 22. "Music stuff is on the right, I think."

Yolonda found the harmonicas stacked between xylophones and an unserious mini set of drums. The harmonicas were boxed and wrapped in cellophane. They cost $4.98. "Two dollars for the box," thought Yolonda. The instrument looked exactly the same as the Kresge one — only four holes. Across the cellophane was stamped in red: PLAYTIME HARMONICA FOR LITTLE MUSICIANS. Might as well boil the Kresge one, thought Yolonda, but she knew that neither harmonica could replace Andrew's old one. She hadn't realized what a good instrument her daddy had given her baby brother. Andrew had been able to get a wide range of notes on it.

It was a real music instrument, thought

Yolonda, and then she realized where she had to go to find the right one. Andrew always watched for the Stellar Musical Instruments display window whenever they drove on Beckmore Drive. But it was a good mile-and-a-half walk from Plaza Mall. She bought a couple of candy bars to help her get there.

Only half the journey had sidewalks. The juice of chewed caramel sluiced sweet and thick around her tongue. And then was gone. What a burg. Most people drove cars in Michigan. Buses didn't run that often, and Yolonda didn't know the schedules or the routes except from her house to the mall. She thought she would die from bored exhaustion walking all the way to Beckmore Drive.

The window at Stellar's held a gleaming set of drums, a bass viol, a portable keyboard, and a saxophone on a stand, all arranged as if musicians had just put them down and gone on a break. Yolonda pushed open the door and went in, suddenly energized.

Guitars galore were hung on walls. She'd never realized there were so many sizes and shapes and colors. A maze of keyboards and drum sets, music stands, horns on stands, and a giant tuba were arranged to divide the space into aisles.

"I want to look at your blues harps," said Yolonda, suddenly deciding that name had a more professional ring than *harmonica*.

"Any kind?" asked the salesclerk, an easy-faced guy with longish gray hair.

Yolonda waited. She didn't know what kind of harmonica, but she knew that waiting sometimes brought discomfort to other people and they would usually fill in the silence with some kind of helpful offering.

"How many reeds? You want twenty? You want a chromatic harp? What key?"

Well, she'd have to answer. "Ten holes," she said. "Key of C. Marine Band."

The man's face lit up. "One of the best basic mouth harps around," he said. "Hohner makes it, of course. Makes most of the good harps." He moved behind a counter in the middle of the store. "You said key of C, yes?"

Yolonda followed, smirking with success.

And there it was — the Marine Band harmonica, just like Andrew's old one, only shiny and unbattered. It came in a little black case with a velvet lining.

"How much?" asked Yolonda.

"This one's eighteen ninety-five."

Yolanda stifled an outcry by holding her breath. "How much without the case?"

"Oh, the case comes with it for free," said the man, smiling.

"Yeah, I bet," said Yolanda sourly. Then she added, "It's for my little brother who's a genius — a musical genius. Anything off for a genius?"

The man had stopped smiling. He looked surprised and amused at the same time. "Not ordinarily," he answered slowly, "but you bring him in sometime to blow me some sounds. I might take five bucks off."

Now it was Yolanda's turn to be surprised. "Yeah? You own this place or something?"

"Something like that," said the man. "Plus I like new sounds."

Yolanda sighed. "I'm not sure I can get my brother here. He's been acting funny ever since he broke his old harmonica. It was a Marine Band one just like this."

"Well, put some bread down on it," said the man. "Bring him in when he's got his stuff together."

"Hold it for eight," said Yolanda, digging into her pocket. "I've got to go home and get the rest." She dumped the money on the counter. "I'll need a receipt for this."

The salesclerk stared at the pile of money.

"It's all there," said Yolonda. "I counted it twice."

"Okay," said the man, and pulled a pen from his shirt pocket. He wrote, "Received on account: $8 toward Marine Band harmonica," and handed the paper to Yolonda.

"Add that there is only six dollars due," said Yolonda, pushing the paper back. She was nobody's fool. "You forgot that part."

"I wouldn't have forgotten that part," said the man. "But I want to hear the kid play. Don't *you* forget that part." He began to add to the receipt. He spoke while writing. "Eight dollars received; six dollars plus tax due upon recital by genius."

"Hurry up," Yolonda told him. "I gotta catch a bus."

After she left, she could feel the gray-haired man watching her through the wide window. She strode out into a power walk, strutting her stuff a little, showing off.

When Yolonda got home that Saturday afternoon, she found Andrew sitting at the piano alone in the house.

"Where's Momma?" asked Yolonda, sliding onto the seat next to him. Probably shopping she thought.

"Shopping," said Andrew.

Yolonda placed her hands gently on the smooth keys. The piano was a power over which she had a questionable control. Since they'd left Chicago, without her Aunt Tiny's interest to inspire her, Yolonda hadn't practiced more than a few times.

"Your Aunt Tiny's piano's going to big waste, Yolonda," her mother was always saying. "Pity she insisted we take it. Tiny thought you'd practice, Yolonda. You could use those good hands of yours for more than pushing food into your mouth."

Yolonda, seated next to Andrew, reached up and opened the music. It was a Mozart sonata, fairly simple except for two horrible trills in the first movement, each a whole finger-lickin' measure long. She could ease into it. She flexed her fingers, shook the blood into her hands, flexed some more, and began to play, slowly letting her fingers press out the notes. She breathed easily like she'd been taught. The notes from the page began to slip into her mind and travel out through her fingers. She rarely had this experience. It was fine. Andrew leaned into her side so gently that her concentration didn't falter. She slowed down only a little for the horrible trills. At the end of the first movement, she stopped. Sighed. She put her arm around Andrew's small shoulders.

"Andrew," she said softly to the top of his head, "why'd you break your harmonica?"

She felt his body go stiff. She rubbed her fingers into his hair, making circles in his scalp the way she used to when he was a baby sitting in her lap. He began to cry.

The knowledge came slowly into her head.

"You didn't break your harmonica, did you?" she asked in relieved surprise. Things began to make sense. "Somebody else broke it." Her relief dwindled, replaced by a deeper guilt.

Andrew nodded, digging his head into her. Yolonda's mind groped through a series of possibilities. Then stopped.

"Asphalt Hill?" she asked.

Andrew nodded.

"Older kid?"

Andrew nodded.

"It wasn't your pal, Karl?"

Andrew shook his head furiously.

No, it wouldn't be Karl, she thought. Nor that Buxton guy.

"Gerard? The white-shirt kid?"

Andrew shook his head.

"The Dudes! It was one of the Dudes!"

Andrew kept very still.

"The Dudes, right? One of those junior-high no-goodniks?"

"Three Dudes," said Andrew, pulling away. He held up three fingers. He looked stricken and frustrated.

In her rising fury, Yolonda recognized that if he had his harmonica, Andrew would play their sound.

From
Dear Mr. Henshaw
by Beverly Cleary

In this Newbery Award–winning novel, Leigh Botts has a lot of mixed-up feelings since his parents have split up. Leigh wrote lots of letters to his favorite author, Boyd Henshaw, and one of the things Mr. Henshaw suggested was for Leigh to write in a diary. Leigh starts each diary entry with "Dear Mr. Pretend Henshaw" since he's used to writing letters, and finds that putting his feelings on paper really helps him sort them out.

Sunday, February 4

Dear Mr. Pretend Henshaw,
   I hate my father.

Mom is usually home on Sunday, but this week there was a big golf tournament, which means rich people have parties, so she had to go squirt deviled crab into about a million little cream puff shells. Mom never worries about meeting the rent when there is a big golf tournament.

I was all alone in the house, it was raining and I didn't have anything to read. I was supposed to scrub off some of the mildew on the bathroom walls with some smelly stuff, but I didn't because I was mad at Mom for divorcing Dad. I feel that way sometimes which makes me feel awful because I know how hard she has to work and try to go to school, too.

I kept looking at the telephone until I couldn't stand it any longer. I picked up the receiver and dialed Dad's number over in Bakersfield. I even remembered to dial 1 first because it was long distance. All I wanted was to hear the phone ringing in Dad's trailer which wouldn't cost Mom anything because nobody would answer.

Except Dad answered. I almost hung up. He wasn't off in some other state. He was in his trailer, and he hadn't phoned me. "You promised to phone me this week and you didn't," I said. I felt I had to talk to him.

"Take it easy, kid," he said. "I just didn't get around to it. I was going to call this evening. The week isn't over yet."

I thought about this.

"Something on your mind?" he asked.

I didn't know what to say, so I said, "My lunch. Somebody steals the good stuff out of my lunch."

"Find him and punch him in the nose," said Dad. I could tell he didn't think my lunch was important.

"I hoped you would call," I said. "I waited and waited." Then I was sorry I said it. I have some pride left.

"There was heavy snow in the mountains," he said. "I had to chain up on Highway 80 and lost time."

From my map book I know Highway 80 crosses the Sierra. I also know about putting chains on trucks. When the snow is heavy, truckers have to put chains on the drive wheels — all eight of them. Putting chains on eight big wheels in the snow is no fun. I felt a little better. "How's Bandit?" I asked, as long as we were talking.

There was a funny silence. For a minute I thought the line was dead. Then I knew something must have happened to my dog. "How's Bandit?" I asked again, louder in case Dad might have lost some of the hearing in his left ear from all that wind rushing by.

"Well, kid —" he began.

"My name is Leigh!" I almost yelled. "I'm not just some kid you met on the street."

"Keep your shirt on, Leigh," he said. "When I had to stop along with some other truckers to put on chains, I let Bandit out of the cab. I thought he would get right back in because it was snowing so hard, but after I chained up, he wasn't in the cab."

"Did you leave the door open for him?" I asked.

Big pause. "I could've sworn I did," he said, which meant he didn't. Then he said, "I whistled and whistled, but Bandit didn't come. I couldn't wait any longer because the highway patrol was talking about closing Highway 80. I couldn't get stranded up there in the mountains when I had a deadline for delivering a load of TV sets to a dealer in Denver. I had to leave. I'm sorry, kid — Leigh — but that's the way it is."

"You left Bandit to freeze to death." I was crying from anger. How could he?

"Bandit knows how to take care of himself," said Dad. "I'll bet dollars to doughnuts he jumped into another truck that was leaving."

I wiped my nose on my sleeve. "Why would the driver let him?" I asked.

"Because he thought Bandit was lost," said Dad, "and he had to get on with his load before the highway was closed, the same as I did. He couldn't leave a dog to freeze."

"What about your CB radio?" I asked. "Didn't you send out a call?"

"Sure I did, but I didn't get an answer. Mountains cut down on reception," Dad told me.

I was about to say I understood, but here comes the bad part, the really bad part. I heard a boy's voice say, "Hey, Bill, Mom wants to know when we're going out to get the pizza." I felt as if my insides were falling out. I hung up. I didn't want to hear any more, when Mom had to pay for the phone call. I didn't want to hear any more at all.

To be continued.

Monday, February 5

I don't have to pretend to write to Mr. Henshaw anymore. I have learned to say what I think on a piece of paper. And I don't hate my father either. I can't hate him. Maybe things would be easier if I could.

Yesterday after I hung up on Dad I flopped down my bed and cried and swore and pounded my pillow. I felt so terrible about Bandit riding around with a strange trucker and Dad taking another boy out for pizza when I was all alone in the house with the mildewed bathroom when it was raining outside and I was hungry. The worst part of all was I knew if Dad took someone to a pizza place for dinner, he wouldn't have phoned me at all, no matter what he said. He would have too much fun playing video games.

Then I heard Mom's car stop out in front. I hurried and washed my face and tried to look as if I hadn't been crying, but I couldn't fool Mom. She came to the door of my room and said, "Hi, Leigh." I tried to look away, but she came closer in the dim light and said, "What's the matter, Leigh?"

"Nothing," I said, but she knew better. She sat down and put her arm around me.

I tried hard not to cry, but I couldn't help it. "Dad lost Bandit," I finally managed to say.

"Oh, Leigh," she said, and I blubbered out the whole story, pizza and all.

We just sat there awhile, and then I said, "Why did you have to go and marry him?"

"Because I was in love with him," she said.

"Why did you stop?" I asked.

"We just got married too young," she said. "Growing up in that little valley town with nothing but sagebrush, oil wells and jackrabbits, there wasn't much to do. I remember at night how I used to look out at the lights of Bakersfield in the distance and wish I could live in a place like that, it looked so big and exciting. It seems funny now, but then it seemed like New York or Paris.

"After high school the boys mostly went to

work in the oil fields or joined the army, and the girls got married. Some people went to college, but I couldn't get my parents interested in helping me. After graduation your dad came along in a big truck and — well, that was that. He was big and handsome and nothing seemed to bother him, and the way he handled his rig — well, he seemed like a knight in shining armor. Things weren't too happy at home with your grandfather drinking and all, so your dad and I ran off to Las Vegas and got married. I enjoyed riding with him until you came along, and — well, by that time I had had enough of highways and truck stops. I stayed home with you, and he was gone most of the time."

I felt a little better when Mom said she was tired of life on the road. Maybe I wasn't to blame after all. I remembered, too, how Mom and I were alone a lot and how I hated living in that mobile home. About the only places we ever went were the laundromat and the library. Mom read a lot and she used to read to me, too. She used to talk a lot about her elementary school principal, who was so excited about reading she had the whole school celebrate books and authors every April.

Now Mom went on. "I didn't think playing

pinball machines in a tavern on Saturday night was fun anymore. Maybe I grew up and your father didn't."

Suddenly Mom began to cry. I felt terrible making Mom cry, so I began to cry some more, and we both cried until she said, "It's not your fault, Leigh. You mustn't ever think that. Your dad has many good qualities. We just married too young, and he loves the excitement of life on the road, and I don't."

"But he lost Bandit," I said. "He didn't leave the cab door open for him when it was snowing."

"Maybe Bandit is just a bum," said Mom. "Some dogs are, you know. Remember how he jumped into your father's cab in the first place? Maybe he was ready to move on to another truck."

She could be right, but I didn't like to think so. I was almost afraid to ask the next question, but I did. "Mom, do you still love Dad?"

"Please don't ask me," she said. I didn't know what to do, so I just sat there until she wiped her eyes and blew her nose and said, "Come on, Leigh, let's go out."

So we got in the car and drove to that fried-chicken place and picked up a bucket of fried chicken. Then we drove down by the ocean and ate the chicken with rain sliding down the windshield and waves breaking on the rocks.

There were little cartons of mashed potatoes and gravy in the bucket of chicken, but someone had forgotten the plastic forks. We scooped up the potato with chicken bones, which made us laugh a little. Mom turned on the windshield wipers and out in the dark we could see the white of the breakers. We opened the windows so we could hear them roll in and break, one after another.

From
In the Year of the Boar and Jackie Robinson
by Bette Bao Lord

10

Fifth grader Shirley Temple Wong has accomplished a lot. She came from China to America and learned to speak English, stood up to a class bully, made a loyal group of friends (including Irvie, who's crazy about spiders), and learned the joys of American baseball.

Now, while Señora Rodriguez — her piano teacher and family's landlady — is visiting her daughter, Nonnie, Shirley has promised to take care of Señora's parrot, Toscanini, and look after the apartment house and collect the rents (with her parents' help). But one big challenge remains: Can Shirley face her fears of the dark basement?

Within the week, Señora Rodriguez was happily on her way to Nonnie. Shirley barely recognized the woman who stepped into the taxi stuffed with suitcases stuffed with gifts. She wore a white linen suit and spectator pumps

85

topped by a straw hat as smart as a lamp-shade. When she waved good-bye, her smile sparkled. A paste of Chinese herbs concocted by Mother had magically coaxed sore gums to adopt the twenty-eight intruders fashioned by the dentist.

Once the taxi disappeared from view, Shirley turned to her parents. "Will it be difficult taking care of this house?"

Father shrugged. "Probably not so difficult as raising a daughter."

"I will help. I promise."

"In that case" — Mother sighed — "kindly refrain from acquiring any more houses for the time being, my little landlord."

"Are you angry with me?"

They laughed. "Not at all. So long as we are collecting rents, we will not have to pay any."

"We're rich! We're rich!"

"Not quite," said Father with that smile. "The first month's rent has already been spent. A surprise for you."

"A whole month's rent just for me?"

"You've earned it."

"What is it? Can I have it now?"

"Patience. It will arrive soon enough."

That night, squeezed into her drawer bed like a stepsister's foot in Cinderella's shoe,

Shirley could hardly sleep thinking of what the surprise might be. Not a piano, please let it not be a piano! The Señora had gone, but Toscanini was left in her care. If it was a piano, she must send a secret letter to China and tattle to the elders about her infamous piano lessons. Surely even a granddaughter who was a singsong girl would not do.

Perhaps it was a lifetime ticket to Ebbets Field? No, her parents would never take her there.

Another engine of some sort? That must be it, she thought. But what kind would be especially made for her? A bicycle? No, not expensive enough. An engine that would match her socks and hang up her clothes? She had never heard of one. A machine that would make strawberry ice cream? Now that would . . . She was asleep.

The surprise was delivered the next afternoon. It looked suspiciously like a sofa. A plain, ordinary sofa just to sit upon. Father must have seen the disappointment on her face, because he quickly cautioned her. "It is not what it seems."

"It isn't?"

After the old sofa was removed and the new one was in place, he told Shirley to stand back and close her eyes.

She did.

When she opened them again, there stood a giant bed fit for an emperor. Shirley threw herself on the mattress and lolled about like a fish tossed back to the sea. "How did you do it, Father? How?"

But before he could say a word, she shouted, "I know. It's just another wonderful engine made in America."

The first Saturday after the departure of the Señora, Shirley sat at the breakfast table hunched over the sports page of the *Herald Tribune*. Her hero had led the Dodgers to extend their winning streak to thirteen games. But what did the writer mean when he warned about the dog days of August?

"Shirley, let's go."

She looked up to see her father dressed in an old pair of pants and an even older shirt. Since he never went anywhere except in a handsome suit and jaunty bow tie, Shirley was surprised.

"Where, Father?"

"To work."

She was more puzzled than ever. Only other engineers understood what her father drew on blue paper. And he never dressed like this for the office.

"Hurry! It's about time we landlords took a good look at the property. We'll start with the furnace room."

Standing in the dimly lit basement while her father tried one key after another, Shirley was glad she was not alone. The strangest noises oozed from behind the locked door. Perhaps Nonnie was not the real reason the Señora had been so anxious to leave. Perhaps there was a monster. One who dined on little girls and had terrible indigestion.

The door creaked open. Father disappeared into the darkness. "I wonder where the light switch is?"

Please let him find it quickly, she prayed. Shirley had to will herself to stay put. Surely that was the flash of the monster's claws! Oh please!

"There, that's better."

The dungeon held no monster, but it was a beastly mess. The walls were stone, dirty and damp. The ceiling was cluttered with pipes that dripped, dripped, dripped and enough spider webs to keep Irvie content for a year. Piled high everywhere was junk, metal skeletons of forgotten species. In one corner stood a black iron box the size of several coffins. In another, huge rusty canisters. Underfoot, pools of murky water slick with oil. Fearing lizards and rats, cockroaches and snakes, Shirley hastened to her father's side.

"Yuck! This is horrible."

But Father did not seem to hear. He grinned as if he had unearthed a store of treasures, banging a pipe here, examining a wire there. "This will be a wonderful challenge. Just wonderful."

Had Father gone loco?

Throughout the game with the Cubs, they worked. Sorting, cleaning, stacking, drying, saving, discarding, boxing. Throughout, Shirley wished she had never heard of Nonnie. She longed for her old drawer bed. The emperor could keep his.

The worst part of it was that Father did not even notice her unhappiness, her goodness. He hummed as he puttered. How could grown-ups be so blind to the pain of those younger and shorter than they? It was not fair.

If only she had a fever, then she could rest. Mother would wait on her, making sweet-and-sour soup and all the things she liked to eat. Father would buy her presents. She could listen to the radio. But she almost never had fevers. So that was that.

"Shirley, come here and help me with this."

"Yes, Father."

It was many evenings and weekends before Shirley realized the treasure her father had mined from the basement. With his alchemy of ingenuity and patience, he transmuted the junk into valued presents for every tenant who lived at Number Four Willow Street. A toaster for Professor Hirshbaum, who knew everything about everything except how to cook. A sewing machine for nearsighted Mrs. O'Reilly, who was forever tailoring old clothes for her triplets, Sean, Seamus and Stephen. A vacuum cleaner for Mr. Habib, who prized his carpets from Persia almost as much as his poodle, Mademoiselle F. P. At one time the initials had stood for Fifi Pompadour, but of late the pet had been known to all who shared the halls as Mademoiselle Faultee Plumbing. A fan for Widow Garibaldi, who now made Father an exception to her rule that men were never, ever to be trusted. An exercise machine for Mr. Lee, the 98-pound weakling.

Meanwhile, in her role of unhappy helper but obedient daughter, Shirley had become quite adept with tools and familiar with the inner workings of the old house. What she could possibly do with her knowledge of the intake valve, the Phillips screwdriver, the temperature cutoff, the ground wire, she did not know. But Father's pride in having raised a handygirl sometimes seemed worth the trouble.

There was one task, however, from which Father excluded her. He was much too meticulous an artist to permit so unsteady a hand to apply even a drop of paint to his hallways.

And so the Goddess Kwan Yin at last showed her mercy. While Father painted the halls a lovely pale beige, Shirley was free to add her howls to the protests against Enos Slaughter of the Cardinals, who had deliberately gone for Jackie Robinson's leg instead of first base and spiked her hero. It was a heartbreaking game, and the Dodgers lost. But Robinson would not be sidelined, and de Bums took the next five. The pennant was within sight.

One evening while Father was out and Shirley was pasting clippings in her Dodgers scrapbook, the lights suddenly went off. Yes, of course, naturally, Mother screamed.

Every tenant was shouting up the stairwell. Mademoiselle yapped. Toscanini squawked. Sean, Seamus and Stephen cried.

Shirley took charge. "Don't worry, Mother. I know just what to do."

"You do? What is it? Do it quickly!"

92

At every turn, Shirley collided with her mother. "Sit down, Mother. I will first go into the kitchen to turn on the stove. Then I will light a candle and change the fuses in the fuse box."

"Fuses? What's fuses?"

"Never mind." Shirley's tone befitted her superior knowledge. "You'll see. Within minutes the lights will all go back on."

"Hurry! Hurry!"

With key ring in one hand and candle in the other, Shirley made her way past the frantic tenants to the basement.

There, she inserted the key into the lock. But as the door swung open, out went the flame. Onto the floor dropped the candle. Vanished, her confidence. It was darker than an underground cave on a moonless night. The familiar noises of the boiler and pipes no longer sounded so innocent, and though she knew spiders and vermin no longer lurked within, she pictured them, multiplied and magnified, waiting to take revenge upon the little landlord who had so callously ousted them from their ancestral homes.

Her legs felt like spaghetti out of a can. The keys jingled in her hand. When she swallowed, it was her heart.

Amitabha! Why had she been so quick to

show off again? Next time, she would hold her tongue. Next time . . . if there ever was a next time.

But done was done. She had to finish what she had started. Just a few steps to the fuse box. She must. She would. She had to.

Pocketing the keys, she felt her way along the walls. Was it her imagination, or did they feel wet and sticky, like blood?

Hand over hand she moved along the walls, stopping at each step to explore the surface, searching for the door to the fuse box. She should have reached it long ago. Who had moved it? If only she had a gourd to ward off the wicked spirits that delight in displacing everyday things. If only she had worn a talisman to ensure her long life. But she was defenseless against all the demons of the dark. Defenseless even against her own thoughts, which told her that the walls were clammy with goo. Goo, like the innards of little girls.

It seemed as if weeks had passed, as if she had inched along the entire length of the Great Wall of China, which the emperor had built to keep out the barbarians, all fifteen hundred miles of it, when she heard her father's voice. "Shirley? Shirley?"

Like a criminal pardoned at the gallows, she ran from the scene, hand over hand, along the walls, up the stairwell. "Father! Father!"

Between the second- and third-floor landing, she fell into his arms. "I thought you might need some help," he said, as matter-of-factly as if saying "Good morning."

Shirley took a deep breath, then waited for her voice to return. "I certainly could have done the job alone. Changing fuses is easy, but maybe with the two of us, it will go quicker."

"Yes, indeed."

With the aid of his cigarette lighter, the mission was accomplished without mishap.

But when the lights returned, Father screamed.

Fearfully, Shirley looked around. Were there monsters after all? But no. To her horror she saw that the sticky goo had been no figment of her imagination. Unbeknownst to her, Father had painted the furnace room and the paint had not yet dried. Now everywhere Shirley looked were little red palm prints—little red palm prints, like a school of exotic fish, swimming down the halls and up the stairwell.

Upon further study, she thought her handiwork rather dazzling. Most original. A masterpiece, even. If only . . . if only the other tenants of Number Four Willow Street could be made to think so too.

But, alas, like that of so many great artists in history, Shirley's genius went unrecognized. Her masterpiece soon lay unseen beneath several new coats of ordinary house paint.

From
Bridge to Terabithia
by Katherine Paterson

In this Newbery Award–winning novel, Jess Aarons, who's always been sort of a loner in his rural Virginia town, meets Leslie Burke. Leslie's from the Washington suburbs. She and her parents seem, well, odd to Jess and his folks. And besides, Leslie's a girl. But Jess and Leslie form a special bond anyway, and Jess's life is never the same again.

Leslie was grinning at him over May Belle's head.

"Well," he said happily. "See you."

"Hey, do you think we could do something this afternoon?"

"Me, too! I wanna do something, too," May Belle shrilled.

Jess looked at Leslie. No was in her eyes. "Not this time, May Belle. Leslie and I got something we gotta do just by ourselves to-day. You can carry my books home and tell Momma I'm over at Burkes'. OK?"

"You ain't got nothing to do. You ain't even planned nothing."

Leslie came and leaned over May Belle, putting her hand on the little girl's thin shoulder. "May Belle, would you like some new paper dolls?"

May Belle slid her eyes around suspiciously. "What kind?"

"Life in Colonial America."

May Belle shook her head. "I want Bride or Miss America."

"You can pretend these are bride paper dolls. They have lots of beautiful long dresses."

"Whatsa matter with 'um?"

"Nothing. They're brand-new."

"How come you don't want 'um if they're so great?"

"When you're my age" — Leslie gave a little sigh — "you just don't play with paper dolls anymore. My grandmother sent me these. You know how it is, grandmothers just forget you're growing up."

May Belle's one living grandmother was in Georgia and never sent her anything. "You already punched 'um out?"

"No, honestly. And all the clothes punch out, too. You don't have to use scissors."

They could see she was weakening. "How about," Jess began, "you coming down and taking a look at 'um, and if they suit you, you could take 'um along home when you go tell Momma where I am?"

After they had watched May Belle tearing up the hill, clutching her new treasure, Jess and Leslie turned and ran up over the empty field behind the old Perkins place and down to the dry creek bed that separated farmland from the woods. There was an old crab tree there, just at the bank of the creek bed, from which someone long forgotten had hung a rope.

They took turns swinging across the gully on the rope. It was a glorious autumn day, and if you looked up as you swung, it gave you the feeling of floating. Jess leaned back and drank in the rich, clear color of the sky. He was drifting, drifting like a fat white lazy cloud back and forth across the blue.

"Do you know what we need?" Leslie called to him. Intoxicated as he was with the heavens, he couldn't imagine needing anything on earth.

"We need a place," she said, "just for us. It would be so secret that we would never tell anyone in the whole world about it." Jess came swinging back and dragged his feet to stop. She lowered her voice almost to a whisper. "It might be a whole secret country," she continued, "and you and I would be the rulers of it."

Her words stirred inside of him. He'd like to be a ruler of something. Even something that wasn't real. "OK," he said. "Where could we have it?"

"Over there in the woods where nobody would come and mess it up."

There were parts of the woods that Jess did not like. Dark places where it was almost like being underwater, but he didn't say so.

"I know" — she was getting excited — "it could be a magic country like Narnia, and the only way you can get in is by swinging across on this enchanted rope." Her eyes were bright. She grabbed the rope. "Come on," she said. "Let's find a place to build our castle stronghold."

They had gone only a few yards into the woods beyond the creek bed when Leslie stopped.

"How about right here?" she asked.

"Sure," Jess agreed quickly, relieved that there was no need to plunge deeper into the woods. He would take her there, of course, for he wasn't such a coward that he would mind a little exploring now and then farther in amongst the ever-darkening columns of the tall pines. But as a regular thing, as a permanent place, this was where he would choose to be — here where the dogwood and redbud played hide-and-seek between the oaks and evergreens, and the sun flung itself in golden streams through the trees to splash warmly at their feet.

"Sure," he repeated himself, nodding vigorously. The underbrush was dry and would be easy to clear away. The ground was almost level. "This'll be a good place to build."

Leslie named their secret land "Terabithia," and she loaned Jess all of her books about Narnia, so he would know how things went in a magic kingdom — how the animals and the trees must be protected and how a ruler must behave. That was the hard part. When Leslie spoke, the words rolling out so regally, you knew she was a proper queen. He could hardly manage English, much less the poetic language of a king.

But he could make stuff. They dragged boards and other materials down from the scrap heap by Miss Bessie's pasture and built their castle stronghold in the place they had found in the woods. Leslie filled a three-pound coffee can with crackers and dried fruit and a one-pound can with strings and nails. They found five old Pepsi bottles which they washed and filled with water, in case, as Leslie said, "of siege."

Like God in the Bible, they looked at what they had made and found it very good.

"You should draw a picture of Terabithia for us to hang in the castle," Leslie said.

"I can't." How could he explain it in a way Leslie would understand, how he yearned to reach out and capture the quivering life about him and how when he tried, it slipped past his fingertips, leaving a dry fossil upon the page? "I just can't get the poetry of the trees," he said.

She nodded. "Don't worry," she said. "You will someday."

He believed her because there in the shadowy light of the stronghold everything seemed possible. Between the two of them they owned the world and no enemy, Gary Fulcher, Wanda Kay Moore, Janice Avery, Jess's own fears and insufficiencies, nor any of the foes whom Leslie imagined attacking Terabithia, could ever really defeat them.

From
Betsy and Tacy Go Over the Big Hill
by Maud Hart Lovelace

Betsy, Tacy, and Tib, best friends for years, are absolutely certain that after Betsy turns ten, it will be time for formal tea parties and elegant speech. Betsy's been looking forward to her birthday for ages, especially since Tacy and Tib have already had theirs. But now she's wondering: What will it really be like to be ten?

In the morning it seemed thrilling to be ten years old.

Betsy jumped out of bed and ran to the window. The lawn, the road, the branches of the trees, and Tacy's roof across the street were skimmed with snow. But she knew it could not last, in April.

"Happy birthday!" said Julia, struggling into her underwear beside the warm chimney which angled up from the hard-coal heater downstairs. She spoke politely. She did not pound Betsy on the back as on other birthday mornings. But Betsy suspected that

Julia was thinking more of the dignity of her own twelve years than of Betsy's ten.

Betsy answered carelessly, "That's right. It *is* my birthday."

She dressed and went humming carelessly down the stairs.

Her father pounded her plenty. And he held her while Margaret pounded. She was pounded and tickled and kissed. Of course it was hard to act careless during such a rumpus, but after it was over Betsy acted careless again. She crooked her finger when she lifted her milk glass, but just a little; she was afraid that Julia would notice.

"Don't you feel well, Betsy?" asked her mother.

"Why, yes," said Betsy. "I feel fine."

"She's very quiet," said her father. "It's the weight of her years."

Betsy was startled until she saw that her father was joking. Her father was a great one to joke.

The pounding and joking showed that her birthday was remembered but still nobody mentioned asking Tacy and Tib to supper. Betsy got ready for school slowly. When her father left for the shoe store, she was still dawdling over her coat and stocking cap, tangling her mitten strings, and losing her rubbers. She gave her mother plenty of chance to bring up the subject. But it didn't do any good.

At last Betsy said, "Hadn't I better ask Tacy and Tib over to supper, Mamma?"

"Not today," answered Mrs. Ray. She sounded for all the world as though any other day would do as well.

"Mamma's pretty busy today. You know Friday's cleaning day," Julia said importantly.

Cleaning day! Betsy could hardly believe her ears.

She tried to act as though it didn't matter.

"When I was only nine I would have teased," she thought.

She kissed her mother good-bye and went humming out the door and across the street to Tacy's.

Mrs. Kelly came to the door and said, "Isn't this your birthday, Betsy?"

"*Indeed* it is," said Betsy, stressing the "indeed" and looking hard at Tacy. Her manner was light and careless, very grown-up.

Mrs. Kelly did not seem to notice the grown-upness. She took Betsy's round red cheeks in her hands and said, "It's five years today that you and Tacy have been friends."

"Goodness!" said Betsy, forgetting to act old for a minute because she *felt* so old.

But she and Tacy acted old all the way down Hill Street, and even more so after they had cut through the vacant lot to Pleasant Street and called for Tib at her beautiful chocolate-colored house. It was fun to watch Tib's round blue eyes grow rounder as she listened to them talk.

"Will you both come to tea some day this week?" Betsy asked carelessly.

"Yes *indeed*," said Tacy. "I'd love to. Wouldn't you, Tib?"

"Um-hum," said Tib.

"When I get some money," said Betsy, "I'm going to buy some nail powder. I'm going to start buffing my nails. I think we all ought to."

"So do I," said Tacy. "I think my sister Mary would lend us a little nail powder, maybe."

"Do you really?" asked Betsy.

"Yes *indeed*," said Tacy. Tacy loved to say "indeed."

Tib didn't know how to talk in the new way. She hadn't learned yet. But she tried.

"I borrowed my mamma's nail powder once and I spilled it," she said.

Betsy and Tacy hurried over that.

"We must buy some hairpins too," said Betsy. "Of course we're not quite ready to put up our hair, but we shall be soon."

"I can hardly wait to get my skirts down," Tacy said. "Ankle length is what I *prefer.*"

"What do you *prefer,* Tib?" asked Betsy.

"I don't know what *'prefer'* means, exactly," said Tib. "Betsy, do you think I still look like a baby?"

Betsy glanced at her and hastily glanced away.

"Not so much as you did yesterday," she said.

"Try to talk like us, Tib," Tacy advised. "It's easy when you get started."

They talked grown-up all the way to school; and they kept on doing it coming home from school at noon, and going back after dinner, and coming home again at three o'clock.

On that trip, when they reached the corner by Tib's house, Betsy felt a strong return of that queer feeling inside. The snow was melting and the ground was slushy and damp. It wasn't a good time for playing out. Today of all days, she should be asking Tacy and Tib to come to her house. And her mother had told her not to!

Tacy and Tib acted embarrassed. Tacy looked at Tib and Tib looked at Tacy and said, "Why don't you come into my house to play?"

"I'd like to. Wouldn't you, Betsy?" Tacy asked.

"There are some funny papers you haven't seen," said Tib. "Is it all right for us to look at them, now we are ten?"

"Of course," said Tacy hastily. "Lots of grown people read the funny papers. Don't they, Betsy?"

"Oh, of course!" Betsy said.

So they went into Tib's house, where they always loved to go; it was so beautiful with a tower on the front and panes of colored glass in the front door. They sat on the window seat and looked at the funny papers, crooking their fingers when they turned the pages. Betsy began to feel better. She had an idea.

"I think we're too old," she said, "to call each other by our nicknames anymore. I think we ought to start using our real names. For instance, you should call me Elizabeth."

"Yes," said Tacy. "And you should call me Anastacia."

"And you should call me Thelma," said Tib. "Hello, Anastacia! How-de-do, Elizabeth?"

The big names made them laugh. Whenever they said "Anastacia" they laughed so hard that they rolled on the window seat.

Matilda, the hired girl, came in from the kitchen.

"What's going on in here?" she asked, looking cross. Matilda almost always looked cross.

"Anastacia and Elizabeth are making me laugh," said Tib.

"No. It's Thelma acting silly," cried Betsy and Tacy.

"Where are all those folks?" asked Matilda, looking around. Betsy, Tacy, and Tib shouted at that.

They had such a good time that Betsy almost forgot how strange it was not to have Tacy and Tib come to supper on her most important birthday. But when the time came to go home she remembered.

"Tacy," she said, as they walked through the vacant lot, "people don't make as much fuss about birthdays after other people grow up. Have you noticed that?"

"Um — er," said Tacy. She acted embarrassed again.

"Not that it matters, of course," said Betsy. "It doesn't matter a bit."

It did, though.

It was dusk when she reached home but no lamps had been lighted except in the kitchen where Mrs. Ray was bustling about getting supper. She wore a brown velvet bow in her high red pompadour and a fresh brown checked apron tied around her slender waist.

Julia was scrubbing Margaret at the basin. And Julia too looked very spic and span.

"Clean up good for supper, Betsy," her mother said.

"Yes, ma'am," said Betsy.

"Mamma," said Julia, "don't you think Betsy ought to put on her new plaid hair ribbons?"

"Yes, that's a good idea," said Mrs. Ray.

"After all, it's her birthday," said Julia, and Margaret clapped her wet hand over her mouth and said, "Oh! Oh!" Margaret was only four years old.

"Probably she thinks Julia is giving something away. Probably she thinks I don't know we'll have a birthday cake," thought Betsy. And then she thought, "Maybe we won't. Things get so different as you get older." She felt gloomy.

But she scrubbed her face and hands. And Julia helped her braid her hair and even crossed the braids in back; they were just long enough to cross. Julia tied the plaid bows perkily over Betsy's ears.

When she was cleaned up, Betsy went into the back parlor. The fire was shining through the isinglass windows of the hard-coal heater there. It looked cozy and she would have enjoyed sitting down beside it with a book. But her mother called out:

"Betsy, I borrowed an egg today from Mrs. Rivers. Will you return it for me, please?"

"Right now?" asked Betsy.

"Yes, please," her mother answered.

"Of all things!" said Betsy to herself.

It seemed to her that she might return the egg tomorrow. It seemed to her that Julia might do the errands on this particular day. It was a nuisance getting into outdoor clothes when she had just taken them off.

"What must I wear?" she asked, trying not to show she was cross because it was her birthday.

"You'll only need your coat and rubbers. Go out the back way," her mother said.

So Betsy put on her coat and rubbers and took an egg and went out the back way.

Mrs. Rivers lived next door, and she was very nice. She had a little girl just Margaret's age, and a still smaller girl, and a baby. The baby was sitting in a high chair eating his supper and Mrs. Rivers asked Betsy to stay a moment and watch him. He was just learning how to feed himself and he was funny.

111

Betsy stayed and watched him. And she said "indeed" and "prefer" to Mrs. Rivers and that cheered her up a little. Mrs. Rivers kept looking out of the window. At last she said:

"I'm afraid your mother will be expecting you now. Good-bye, dear. Go out the back way."

So Betsy went out the back way and climbed the little slope which led to her house. The ground was slippery, for the melted snow had frozen again. The stars above the hill were icy white.

She went into the house dejectedly. There was no one in the kitchen. The door which led to the dining room was closed.

"They've started supper without me. On my birthday!" Betsy thought. She felt like sitting down and crying.

She opened the dining room door and then stopped. No wonder she stopped! The room was crowded with children. They called, "Surprise! Surprise! Surprise on Betsy!"

Betsy's father stood there with his arm around Betsy's mother and both of them were smiling. Tacy and Tib rushed over to Betsy and began to pound her on the back, and Julia ran into the front parlor and started playing the piano. Everybody sang:

"Happy birthday to you!
Happy birthday to you!
Happy birthday, dear Betsy,
Happy birthday to you!"

"It's a surprise party," cried Margaret, red-faced from joyful suspense.

It was certainly a surprise.

There were ten little girls at the party because Betsy was ten years old. Ten little girls, that is, without Margaret, who was too little to count. Betsy made one, and Julia made two, and Tacy made three, and Katie made four, and Tib made five, and a little girl named Alice who lived down on Pleasant Street made six, and Julia's and Katie's friend Dorothy who also lived down on Pleasant Street made seven, and three little girls from Betsy's class in school made eight, nine, and ten.

There were ten candles on the birthday cake, but before they had the birthday cake they had sandwiches and cocoa; and along with the birthday cake they had ice cream; and after the birthday cake they played games in front and back parlors. Betsy's father played with them; Betsy's mother played the piano for Going to Jerusalem; and when Betsy's father was left without a chair how everybody laughed!

Betsy and Tacy and Tib played harder than anyone. They forgot to crook their fingers and to say "indeed" and "prefer." They forgot to call one another Elizabeth and Anastacia and Thelma. In fact, after that day, they never did these things again.

But just the same, in the midst of the excitement, Betsy realized that she was practically grown-up.

Flushed and panting from Blind Man's Buff, her braids loose, and her best hair ribbon untied, she found her mother.

"Mamma," she said, "this is the first party I ever had at night."

"That's right," her mother answered. "The children are staying until nine o'clock, and Papa is taking them home."

"Is it because I'm ten years old?" asked Betsy.

"Of course it is," her mother answered.

Betsy rushed to find Tacy and Tib. She drew them into a corner.

"You notice," she whispered proudly, "that we're having this party at night."

"What about it?" asked Tib.

"What about it?" repeated Betsy. "Why, it's a grown-up party."

"It's practically a ball," said Tacy.

"Oh," said Tib.

"Of course," she pointed out after a moment, "tomorrow isn't a school day."

Tib always mentioned things like that. But Betsy and Tacy liked her just the same.

From
My Life as a Fifth-Grade Comedian
by Elizabeth Levy

Bobby Garrick is the class clown. To keep him from causing trouble, the principal has allowed Bobby to organize a students versus teachers joke contest. Now the Great Laugh-Off has begun. Bobby's edged out all the other students and he's up against his favorite teacher in the final round. Bobby's learned a lot about using humor carefully so that he doesn't hurt others the way his dad's sarcasm so often hurts him. But has he learned enough to win this last stand-up standoff?

I listened to the end of Mr. Matous's routine. He was pretty funny, but most of his jokes were kind of the same as his first set. "The kids in my class need a little help with their grammar," he said. "Sometimes I give them examples of improper English and ask them to correct it. I wrote on the board, 'I didn't have no fun at the seashore' and asked, 'How should I fix this?' 'Get a date,' shouted Bobby

116

Garrick." It had happened way in the beginning of the year. I had completely forgotten about it.

I stopped listening to him. I had to think about my own routine. Everything felt so mixed up. Jokes were easier for me when I knew exactly how I felt about everybody. Grandma was nice; Dad was mean; Mom was scared of her own shadow; and my brother was a screwup. How was I supposed to win the Great Laugh-Off if nobody stayed the same? Who was I supposed to make fun of? I knew the answer: Me.

I heard Mr. Matous say, "Thank you all very much."

Mr. Matous came offstage. He looked like he had just swum the English Channel all by himself. "Okay, Bobby, it's your turn. Just remember, right now there's no such thing as being too funny."

I took the stage. My heart was pounding. I felt totally out of control. I forced myself to breathe as I looked out across the bright lights. I took the microphone, and my hands were so sweaty, the microphone flew into the air. I juggled it. There was a titter of nervous laughter. I was dying inside. I could feel the audience staring at me. They weren't sure whether to laugh or not. The entire audience grew silent.

I was drenched in sweat. I was bombing right in front of their eyes. I could see Dad in the audience. He looked so nervous.

I scratched my head. "The head lice in my hair are coming out to rescue me any minute," I said. "Those little buggers never forget a joke."

The audience laughed loudly. They were with me again. They had remembered the joke from my first routine. I had done a callback. Now I had a choice. I could keep going making safe jokes about bugs, or I could go for the jugular. All great comics have to go for the jugular.

"My dad has this habit," I said. There was a pause. I could tell people were on edge. What was I going to say? Was I going to reveal something really embarrassing about Dad — something that nobody wanted to hear?

"He loves to ask questions that you should never answer. All adults do this, but my dad is a perfectionist about it. A perfectionist is someone who takes infinite pains to get something right — but in my dad's case it means he gives everyone around him infinite pains in the butt . . . specially my mom, me and my brother."

I could hear Jimmy laughing harder than anybody. A lot of the kids and teachers knew

118

about Jimmy and me always getting into trouble, but even the ones who didn't were laughing. The kids were catching on that it was okay to laugh at your parents and your family today.

I looked out at the audience, and Dad was looking up at me. "My dad is always asking me, 'Where are your manners?'" I paused. The audience laughed — but a little anxiously. "Does he think I know where my manners are?" I blurted out. "Gee, Dad, they were here a few minutes ago, but they've gone to Disney World. They'll send you a postcard. It'll be a very, very polite postcard. 'Dear Bobby's parents, Thank you for the lovely stay at your house with Bobby. But we won the Superbowl of Manners, and we got to go to Disney World. Wish you were here!'"

I got a laugh with that one. It just came rolling in on me — a gigantic wave of sound. I fiddled with the microphone. I thought the audience would get restless, but they seemed willing to wait for me. I swallowed and tried not to look at Dad, but it was hard. My eyes kept going back to him.

"Here's another question that my dad likes to ask: 'How many times do I have to tell you this?' Keep going, Dad, you're near the record.

"You know, Dad also seems to have an obsession with the idea that my friends are all going to jump off a bridge. 'If the other kids all jumped off a bridge, would you jump?' It's one of his favorite questions. How can I answer that? Oh yeah, Dad. I just came home to get my bathing suit."

The laughs were pouring in now. All the kids who had to listen to their parents ask them these dumb questions were howling their heads off.

I nodded and grinned. "I mean, where do parents *get* these questions? Do they get an instruction manual when we're born? Here, ask these questions, and you'll drive your kids crazy."

I looked out again. Dad and Grandma were both cracking up. Even Mom had a real smile on her.

I was making fun of Dad, but not of myself. I looked out at the audience. "Changing is hard," I blurted out. "Doing it up here on-stage — it's like trying to suck a dinosaur up your nose." I knew the audience didn't exactly know what I meant, but they were with me. They would follow me anywhere. I took a deep breath. I was flying without a net.

"See, I should tell the truth. I was born with an instruction manual on how to drive my parents and all adults crazy. Just before I was delivered, a little voice whispered into my ear — 'Bobby, be a joker.'

"I think kids and adults are programmed to drive each other nuts. Kids are born just knowing that someday we'll get to yell at our parents, 'How come you're so mean?' If that doesn't get them, I always try, 'Don't you remember what it's like to be a little kid?' Well, guess what I just found out? My dad does remember what it's like to be a kid. He wishes he could forget — but he can't. I guess the good parents can't forget."

My dad had a funny look on his face.

"See, Dad," I shouted out. "There's really no such thing as being too funny!"

"You're right!" my dad shouted back.

There was a silence from the audience. Dad's answer had broken my comic routine. But I knew what Dad was trying to tell me. He was telling me that no matter what happened with the Great Laugh-Off, we had both won a much bigger contest.

I scratched my head. "Gee, Dad," I said. "You even got my head lice jumping with that one. Now I'm sorry I put some of these little buggers on your pillow last night." I shrugged and looked sheepishly out at the audience. "Just kidding!" Dad was laughing so hard, tears were running down his face.

I was nearly done. I looked out at the audience. I played it straight. "Now, I've got one last question for you — What's too funny for our own good? I think the answer is: nothing. Nothing is *too* funny, and there's enough funny stuff for all of us."

I took a bow. Sweat was running down my armpits and my back. I almost couldn't breathe. I gulped. I felt like my insides were melting away. I wiped my eyes. I hadn't been funny. I was sure I had been too serious, but kids were stamping their feet and cheering! Maybe they were just glad that I had finally left the stage.

Ms. Lofti came out onstage with Mr. Matous and Dr. Deal. "Girls and boys," said Ms. Lofti. "As the official laugh-a-meter for the Great Laugh-Off, I declare that the final laugh-off has been won — by Bobby Garrick. Let's give him a big round of applause. Bobby, you've won a month's supply of pizza, and this trophy!"

I stared at the trophy. Mr. Matous handed it to me. It was a giant gold cup, the kind you see locked up in cases in the hallway at school — that's how big it was. I looked inside, and sitting in there was a giant jar of Vaseline. I started to laugh. "I got it in case you won," Matous whispered.

122

I took the Vascline out and waved it in the air. "A joker's best friend!" I shouted. My class cracked up.

I saw Grandma and Mom and Dad standing up in the first row.

I took the microphone. "Thank you, everybody," I said. "I want to thank my grandmother, who has always laughed at my jokes; my brother, who taught me my first knock-knock joke; and my mom, who's responsible for this tie." I waved its ends in the air. The audience laughed, and Mom looked pleased.

"But most of all, I want to really thank my dad. Once I got mad at him when he said that I got my sense of humor from him. But now I've got to say thank you, Dad. I think I did."

Then I did something that I never thought I would do. I jumped off the stage. I went to where my dad was sitting. I took his hand. He shook his head, but I tugged at him, and brought him up onstage. Later Janeen said she wanted me up on the stage all by myself, but see, I know something. I'm going to get plenty of chances to be up there by myself — but this was a time I wanted Dad up there with me — to let him know that I loved him and that he was funny too.

From
The Kid in the Red Jacket
by Barbara Park

Howard is the new kid in school. He misses his best friends, Thornsberry and Roger, but he is determined to make friends. There's just one problem: Howard's first-grade neighbor, Molly, thinks she's Howard's most important new friend. Howard isn't crazy about having a six-year-old sidekick — he's afraid it'll ruin his reputation — but he's finding that letting Molly down doesn't feel so good.

My father gave me some advice. He's tried this kind of thing before, but it's never worked out too well. The trouble is, most of the time his advice is about stuff he doesn't know how to do. Like during basketball season, he'll tell me how to shoot a lay-up. Then he'll shoot a lay-up and miss. It's hard to take advice like that.

"Horn in," he said one night at dinner. I was explaining how much I hated to eat lunch alone, and he looked right up from his pork chop and said, "Horn in."

"Er, horn in?" I repeated, confused. I guess it must be one of those old-time expressions they don't use much anymore.

"Sure. Be a little pushy. Stand up for yourself," he went on. "You can't wait for the whole world to beat a path to your door."

"Beat a path to my door?" I asked again. Another old-time expression, I think.

"That means you can't wait for everyone else to come to you, son," he explained. "Sometimes you've just got to take the bull by the horns."

"Oh geez. Not more horns," I groaned.

"Bull by the horns," repeated Dad. "Haven't you ever heard that before? It means you've got to get right in there and take charge. If you don't want to eat alone, then sit right down at the lunch table with the rest of them. Just walk up there tomorrow, put your lunch on the table, and say, 'Mind if I join you, fellas?' That's all there is to it."

I didn't say anything, but kids just don't go around talking like that. If a kid came up to a bunch of guys eating lunch and said, "Mind if I join you, fellas?" the whole table would fall on the floor laughing.

Still, I knew what Dad was getting at. I think it's something all new kids learn sooner or later. Even if you're the shy type, you have to get a little bold if you want to make any friends. You have to say hi and talk to people, even if it makes you nervous. Sometimes you even have to sit down at a lunch table without being invited. You don't have to say, "Mind if I join you, fellas?" though. I'm almost positive of that.

I have to admit that the "horning in" part worked out pretty well. The next day at lunch I took a deep breath, sat down at the table with the other guys, and started eating. That was that. No one seemed to mind, really. They hardly even stared.

After that it got easier. Once kids have seen you at their table, it's not as hard to accept you the next time. Then pretty soon they figure that you must belong, or you wouldn't be sitting there every day.

I'm not saying that after horning in I automatically started to love Rosemont, Massachusetts; or that I still didn't think about Thornsberry and Roger every single day. All I mean is, the more days that passed, the less I felt like an outsider. I guess you'd say stuff started feeling more familiar. Like at school, if a stranger had asked me for directions, I could have steered him to all the water fountains and lavatories. For some reason, knowing your lavatories sort of gives you a feeling of belonging.

I guess moving to a new school is like anything else you hate. Even though you can't stand the thought of it, and you plan to hate it for the rest of your life, after you've been doing it for a while, you start getting used to it. And after you start getting used to it, you forget to hate it as much as you'd planned. I think it's called adjusting. I've given this some thought, and I've decided that adjusting is one of those things that you can't control that much. It's like learning to like girls. It sort of makes you nauseous to think about it, but you know it's going to happen.

By the end of the second week, most of the kids in my class knew my name. They didn't use it that much, but when the teacher said, "Yes, Howard?" they turned around and looked. So I know they knew.

There was still a big problem in my life, though. Very big. And you spelled it M-O-L-L-Y. She was coming over to "play" with me more and more. It was getting totally out of control.

I used to think that if you didn't want

someone at your house, getting rid of them would be easy. You could just shout, "Go home!" and that would be that. It doesn't work that way in real life, though. The only time you can feel good about shouting "go home" is when you've had a big fight with someone or if you hate that person's guts.

That was the trouble with Molly. She was kind of a funny little kid, really, and her guts were getting harder to hate. And even if they weren't, my mother kept reminding me of all the mean divorce stuff that had happened to her. It was supposed to make me "think twice" about doing something mean to her.

Still, I found it hard letting her come over every day. After all, a guy has his reputation to think of. And like I said, once word spreads that you're hanging around with first-graders, it's hard to live it down.

I tried to talk to my mother about it, but the conversations were too short to do much good. Mostly she'd just find me hiding behind the couch while Molly was knocking, and she'd make me go to the door. "Stop being stupid and let Molly in," shc'd snap.

Finally, one afternoon before Molly came over, I decided to just tell my mother the whole truth and get it over with. Maybe she'd yell and maybe she wouldn't, but something had to be done.

She was about to put Gaylord down for his nap when I stopped her in the hall.

"It's going to kill me," I announced.

"What's going to kill you?"

"Being friends with Molly. It's going to kill me. You asked me if it would kill me to be nice to her and the answer is yes. I'm sorry. But it will."

My mother held Gaylord with one hand and put the other hand sternly on her hip. "How?" she demanded sharply. "How will it kill you, Howard?"

I was prepared for her to ask her question. "The pressure. You don't know how much pressure I'm under as a new kid. I'm trying to make these great friends, and every day Molly's standing at my front door for the whole world to see. I practically have to yank her in the house so no one will notice. Don't you get it? Kids are beginning to know me now, and I just can't risk it."

"Risk it? Risk *what*, Howard?"

I took a deep breath. This wasn't going to be easy, but I had to try to make her understand.

"Risk being turned into another Ronald

129

Dumont," I admitted reluctantly. "Ronald Dumont was this weirdo at my old school who didn't have any friends his own age, so he ended up playing with the little kids all the time. He whinnied, Mom. I'm not kidding. He actually went around playing horses and whinnying. And after a while all we did was make fun of him."

"Oh, for heaven's sake, Howard. You're not actually afraid that just because Molly comes over here once in a while, you're going to turn into another Ronald Du —"

"Yes, I am!" I interrupted. "Why don't you understand? I mean, I don't think I'm going to start whinnying or anything. But I *am* afraid that kids will think there's something wrong with me. They've already seen her walking to school with me. I'm practically positive. No one's said anything, but I know they've seen us together. The next thing you know, they'll start thinking that I don't fit in with them. Then pretty soon I won't. And before long I'll be out on the playground, tossing my head around like a wild stallion."

My mother stared at me for about ten minutes. Well, actually it was probably more like ten seconds. But the expression on her face made it seem a lot longer.

Finally she just shook her head disgustedly. "I can't believe you're serious. I can't believe you are so worried about what people will think that you can't be nice to a little girl who needs a friend. And what's more, I can't honestly believe that you think being nice to her will turn you into some kind of misfit. But I'm not going to argue with you about this anymore. I'm tired of it, Howard. I'm tired of you hiding behind the couch; and I'm tired of making you go to the door; and I'm tired of trying to make you understand how much she's been through. I'm not going to push her on you anymore, Howard. You do what you want about her. You handle it your own way. But just think about one thing: Someday *you* may need a friend. Not want one. *Need* one. And if you do, you'd better hope that you'll find someone who has a bigger heart than you do."

She didn't understand. I *knew* she wouldn't, and she didn't.

"Hey! Let me in!"

I rolled my eyes. Molly was kicking at the front door, hollering her usual greeting.

My mother stood there, waiting to see what I would do. I hate it when she watches me like that. It's like I'm on trial or something.

"I'll let her in, okay?" I said, annoyed.

Then, without wasting any more time, I reached outside and yanked her in as quickly as I could.

My mother just sighed and walked away.

Molly's hands were spilling over with coloring books and crayons. She'd been coming over to color a lot lately. At first it really bothered me. But then I decided that letting a kid color at your house isn't really the same thing as being her friend. When the painters come and color my walls, I don't consider them my pals or anything.

Sometimes she wanted me to color with her. Usually I didn't. But once in a while I did a page. Just for the heck of it, you know. I'm not exactly too old to color, but almost. I guess you could say I'm right on the coloring border.

Molly really loved it, though. The funny thing was, most of the time she only used lavender and lime-green. Even for skin, she'd color it either lavender or lime-green. Once, when she was coloring a pig, I handed her this color called light pink. She didn't even look up from her book. "I only like lavender and lime-green," she informed me.

"Yeah, I know. But pigs aren't lime-green. You need different colors in your pictures to make them look *real.*"

Molly stopped what she was doing and

132

stared up at me. "It's just pretend, Howard. My nonny says pretend can be any color you want."

Then, for just a split second, she got another one of those sad expressions. "Besides," she added, "I don't always like real."

Sometimes I wondered how she did it. How did she go around acting so happy when there was all that hurt still inside her? Even I wasn't any good at stuff like that. And she was only six.

Anyway, as she sat there coloring, the telephone rang. I didn't bother to answer it. When you're a new kid, the telephone is never for you. I guess that's why when my mother shouted, "Howard! It's for you!" I felt sort of nervous and excited at the same time.

"For me?" I asked, jumping right up. "I hardly even know anyone here."

Molly thought it over for a second. "Maybe it's your teacher calling to tell you that she saw you bump Frankie Boatwright off the seesaw and you can't teeter-totter anymore."

I rolled my eyes. "I didn't bump Frankie Boatwright."

"I didn't either," replied Molly matter-of-factly. "He just wasn't holding on tight enough, that's all." Then she frowned. "It's not my fault he had slippery fingers."

"*Howard!* Are you going to get the phone or not?"

I hurried to my mother's bedroom and picked up the receiver.

"H-h-hello?"

"Hey, Howard. It's Ollie. Ollie Perkins. From school, you know?"

I was almost too happy to answer. A kid! A regular kid my own age calling me at home! Calling me by my name and everything! It was like a miracle!

"Er, yeah, hi, Ollie. What's up?" I managed to say, trying to sound casual.

I was so excited, I can't remember the rest of the conversation. All I know is that some of the kids were setting up a football game on Saturday, and Ollie asked me if I could make it.

Could I make it? Was he kidding? Of course I could make it! This was just the kind of break a new kid prays for.

"*Yeehaa!* A football game!" I shrieked as I hung up the phone. "Some guys are getting a football game together, and they want me to play!"

My mother ran into the room and ruffled my hair. "See? I told you things would get better, didn't I?"

"Me too!" Molly chimed in. "I told you that too! Remember, Howard Jeeper?"

"Yeah, I remember," I replied, still grinning. "You told me."

"Hey!" she said then. "When is it, anyway? I can come, right? I like football, I think. Yup, I'm pretty sure I do."

The grin left my face in a flash. I should have known this would happen. I never should have mentioned the game in front of her.

I looked hopelessly at my mother. Not much help there. She gave me one of those "Now what are you going to do?" expressions and left the room.

I think this was the part I was supposed to handle.

From
Amy and Laura
by Marilyn Sachs

What really counts in a best friend? Amy Stern's been handed a class assignment that's really making her stop and think about that. And as much as she'd like to talk it over with her big sister, Laura, Amy's going to have to figure this one out on her own.

Mrs. Malucci began handing out sheets of yellow paper. Another composition! Amy nearly groaned out loud.

"Now today," Mrs. Malucci said, "I want you all to write a composition on — let me see — on 'My Best Friend.' I hope it will be a better set of papers than the ones you did on Tuesday." Mrs. Malucci looked around the classroom in disgust. "It seems to me that there are very few children in this class who realize that there are other marks of punctuation in the English language besides the period." She looked right at Amy. "Amy Stern," she said, "can you tell the class some other punctuation marks?"

"Yes, Mrs. Malucci," Amy said rising, and smiling. This was easy. "There is the question mark, the comma, the apostrophe, and, uh —"

"Yes," said Mrs. Malucci, "and not one of those you mentioned appeared on your last composition. Yours was the worst in that respect." A relieved titter broke from the class, and Amy bit her lip. "Although," Mrs. Malucci continued mercilessly, looking around the room and quelling the happy sound, "I wasn't satisfied with anybody else's paper either. Now start working, and try to think about what you're doing for a change."

Amy sat down feeling disgraced and abandoned. Why was it people always said married teachers who had children of their own understood children better than single teachers? Mrs. Malucci was married. It was said she even had five children, possibly six. So why didn't she understand children? Why did she always say mean things to children, in front of the whole class too? Amy remembered the composition she had written on Tuesday very well. The subject was "A Funny Story," and she had written such a funny story, such a *long*, funny story too. Why, she had even needed two sheets of paper, and she had nearly laughed out loud as she was writing it. She had been positive Mrs. Malucci would think it was wonderful, but no, count on Mrs. Malucci always to find something nasty to say.

She heard a very faint tapping on the desk next to hers and turned to meet Rosa's sympathetic face. Rosa smiled encouragingly, carefully pointed with her pencil to the paper on her desk, and then, with the pencil, pointed toward Amy. A great happiness rose in Amy's chest. Rosa meant that she was going to say on her paper that Amy Stern was her best friend.

Well! Amy took up her own pencil and settled herself over the empty paper on her desk. "My Best Friend — Rosa Ferrara," she thought in her mind.

"Please, Mrs. Malucci," came a voice from the back, "can I sharpen my pencil?"

"*May* I sharpen my pencil, Henry," corrected Mrs. Malucci. "Come on, then!"

Everybody watched as Henry clumped to the front of the room, ground his pencil in the sharpener, and clumped back to his seat. Then, slowly, the rows of backs bent over the rows of papers on desks.

"Rosa Ferrara has the most beautiful

black braids in the world," Amy thought to herself, pushing her pencil through her own despised blond, frizzy curls. Her blue eyes narrowed on the empty paper as she prepared to fill it with words.

"Mrs. Malucci, *may* I please sharpen my pencil too?"

All thinking about "My Best Friend" halted as forty-three pairs of eyes settled on Mrs. Malucci's face.

"Come, come!" said Mrs. Malucci irritably, "and if anybody else needs to sharpen his pencil, he had better do it right now."

Cynthia marched to the front of the classroom, and a few other children followed. The whirring of the sharpener began again, stopped, and began again. As Cynthia passed Amy's desk on her way back to her seat, she stuck out her tongue and pointed right at Amy with her pencil and then at the empty sheet of paper on Amy's desk.

Well! Was Cynthia actually going to write that she, Amy, was her best friend? And all the time she had supposed that Cynthia considered Annette de Luca her best friend. Of course, for the past two weeks Cynthia and Annette had been mad at each other and weren't even talking. But still! Amy glowed with contentment.

And then the horror of her predicament struck her. Desperately she glued her eyes on the last of the pencil sharpeners, watched him as he returned to his seat, saw the rhythmic lines of backs bent over their work, and her skinny little face wrinkled with her problem.

Who was her best friend anyway? Was it Cynthia or was it Rosa? She wished somebody would tell her. If only Laura were here! But then, she knew very well Laura's opinion on the subject. Laura couldn't stand Cynthia and considered her a bad influence on Amy. Which was sort of a compliment, since it meant that Laura felt there was somebody in the world worse than Amy. Generally, Laura didn't approve of any of Amy's friends. But she did like Rosa. "A nice, quiet little girl with good manners," she said.

Amy liked Rosa too, but not because she was a nice, quiet little girl with good manners. She liked her because she was fun to be with in spite of her good manners and quiet ways. Rosa was especially fun to be with on cold or rainy days when they played indoors. If they played at Rosa's house, which Amy preferred, they could dress up in the beautiful clothes that Rosa's family used to wear when they lived in Puerto Rico. Then, if nobody was in the living room, they could turn on the radio and hunt for some appropriate music. Sad music was best, because they liked to act out sad stories. Rosa was such a magnificent actress that she always carried Amy breathlessly along with her into the story they were acting. Like the time Rosa played the part of a mother whose child was very sick, and Amy was the nurse. The child had suddenly taken a turn for the worse.

"I'm sorry," Amy said sadly, handing back the doll, wrapped in a blanket. "We've done everything we could for him. It's too late."

On that day the music had been especially suitable. Just as Amy spoke, a low beating of drums began.

Rosa's trembling hands reached for the child. She pressed her lips to its cold forehead and dropped to her knees. Back and forth she rocked, crooning to it in Spanish.

"You have other children," Amy said solemnly. "They need you."

But the grief-stricken figure at her feet crouched over the child, kissing it and pleading with it to come back.

There was a lump in Amy's throat as she knelt beside Rosa, and implored her, "Be brave!"

Then the moaning started, low and broken, as the mother rocked backward and forward, the dead child in her arms, and tears, real tears, flowing down her cheeks.

Amy gasped, and began sobbing herself. And the two of them huddled over the poor lost baby, weeping uncontrollably until the music stopped and the commercial began.

If they played at Amy's house, which Rosa preferred, they generally crayoned, or played Chinese Checkers or Monopoly. And because Laura held such a high opinion of Rosa, sometimes she might even condescend to play with them if she had nothing better to do. And the afternoon would pass quietly and pleasantly.

But on fine days, something inside Amy hungered for Cynthia. Nobody could rollerskate so swiftly and so noisily as Cynthia. Nobody could dream up such dangerous expeditions as Cynthia. And nobody could fight so well or talk so fresh as Cynthia.

Amy nibbled on her pencil, and suddenly became aware of Mrs. Malucci's eyes on her. Quickly she crouched low over her desk, hiding behind the back in front of her. Out of the corner of her eye, she watched Rosa turn the paper on her desk and begin writing on the other side.

Jerry Kerner held up his hand for another sheet of paper. Amy looked at the empty paper on her own desk and felt like crying. She just could not decide. And if she did decide on one or the other, what would she do when the other one, the one she had not chosen, asked her what she had written?

"Just start writing," she told herself. "Write anything." But her pencil poised motionlessly above the paper. "Rosa, write Rosa!" she said to herself. "You know she's really your best friend — not just when she's mad at somebody, but all the time." And it was true. Rosa never made fun of her the way Cynthia often did. Never said she was a coward or skinny or disgusting. Rosa never pushed her around or whispered secrets in somebody else's ear about her. "Write Rosa!" she said to herself.

But there were other thoughts too: of high adventure in Crotona Park, of the glory when she followed after Cynthia in scaling Indian Rock and driving off their foes, of the feel of her palm stinging when Cynthia played handball with her in the schoolyard, of the joy when Cynthia whispered in her ear about somebody else.

Rosa put her pencil down, leaned back in

her seat, and smiled over at Amy. All around her, Amy could hear the rustling sound of children finished with their work.

"I have to write something — anything," she thought desperately. "I know, I know. I won't write about either of them." Frantically she began.

MY BEST FRIEND A LONG TIME AGO

A long time ago, before I lived here, I lived in another neighborhood, and my best friend there was a girl named Celia Gerber.

"All right, class," said Mrs. Malucci, "pass your papers forward."

Later that afternoon, Amy stood outside the school waiting for Laura. In her notebook was an empty sheet of paper on which she was to bring back tomorrow a "decent" composition about "My Best Friend." Mrs. Malucci had made some other remarks about people who are lazy, and people who daydream, and people who won't follow instructions. Amy was reviewing these different comments in her mind, and thinking that Mrs. Malucci was not really fair at all.